PENGUIN BOOKS

Electric City and Other Stories

Patricia Grace was born in Wellington in 1937. She is of Ngati Raukawa, Ngati Toa and Te Ati Awa descent, and is affiliated to Ngati Porou by marriage. She has taught in primary and secondary schools in the King Country, Northland and Porirua. She now lives in Plimmerton. She is married with seven children.

Patricia Grace's stories have been published in a number of periodicals and anthologies. Her first collection of stories, *Waiariki*, was published in 1975 (the first collection of stories by a Maori woman writer), and a second collection, *The Dream Sleepers*, in 1980. Her first novel, *Mutuwhenua, The Moon Sleeps*, was first published in 1978. She has also written two children's books, illustrated by Robyn Kahukiwa, *The Kuia and the Spider* (1981) and *Watercress Tuna and the Children of Champion Street* (1985), the former winning the Children's Picture Book of the Year award in 1982. She also wrote the text for *Wahine Toa* (1984), illustrated by Robyn Kahukiwa. Her second novel, *Potiki*, was published in 1986 and placed third equal in the Wattie Book of the Year Award in that year.

Electric City
AND OTHER STORIES

Patricia Grace

PENGUIN BOOKS

Penguin Books (N.Z.) Ltd, 182–190 Wairau Road,
Auckland 10, New Zealand
Penguin Books Ltd, Harmondsworth,
Middlesex, England
Penguin Books, 40 West 23rd Street,
New York, N.Y.10010, U.S.A.
Penguin Books Australia Ltd, Ringwood,
Victoria, Australia
Penguin Books Canada Limited, 2801 John Street,
Markham, Ontario, Canada L3R 1B4

First published 1987

Copyright © Patricia Grace, 1987

Designed by Richard King
Typeset in Compugraphic California
by Edsetera Book Productions Ltd
in association with Typocrafters Ltd, Auckland
Printed in Hong Kong

To my mother

Contents

Waimarie

Waimarie called to Max to come and unplug the iron. She spoke in their own language.

And she told him to have a smoke now, where she could see him. 'Lucy's picking me up,' she said, 'and don't you smoke while I'm out, putting the place on fire. And don't cook. You come down the marae after and have a kai down there, you hear me . . . Get me up,' she said.

For a moment Max stood and looked at her. He had the cigarette out of the packet but he hadn't lit it.

'Get me up,' his sister said again.

So he moved to the settee where she was sitting and took her by the arm, pushing up under her elbow until she stood.

'My stick.'

He unhooked her stick from the back of the settee and put it in her hand.

'Now you do what I say,' she said, and pointed at the tea-towels and tablecloths. 'Put them in the drawer.'

Max put his cigarette down and went to do as she told him.

'And those in the cupboard.' She poked her stick at towels and pillowcases.

'Nothing else,' she said, when he had put the linen away. 'You have your smoke now before Lucy come.'

She picked up Keriata's and Ariana's jeans and tee-shirts and took them to put in their drawer. She put her skirt away and hung Max's shirt on the end of his bed, moving slowly to and fro.

Then she changed into her black dress, and while she was waiting for Lucy she hooked long shark-tooth earrings onto her ears.

'Hot,' Lucy said, as she helped her aunt to stand. 'But could get cold.'

'My shawl, there on the settee,' said Waimarie. 'And my bag too. And dear, I want my teeth, in the bathroom, in the glass.'

'You finish your smoke?' she asked Max, 'You put it out properly?'

He showed her the ashtray with the cigarette butt and the dead match in it.

'Empty that in the rubbish,' she said. 'Wash it, and don't turn on any stove or jug. Don't you smoke. Don't cook nothing. And you wait here. When those girls come back you tell them Nanny gone to the marae. Tell them come straight down. Now, what you going to say to Ariana and Keriata?'

'Nanny gone marae,' he said.

'What else?'

'You go down.'

'Straight down.'

'Straight down.'

'And you speak English, don't forget. Speak English or they won't know.'

On their way down the path Lucy said, 'Your garden's good, Aunt.'

So Waimarie stopped and pointed here and there.

'See all my portulaca, Harriet give me it from her old place but not the dark one, the dark one it's from my mate down the road. She got a big one at the back of her place. The yellow one, it's from Robert's wife. And begonia? I get two when I'm in the hospital and when I come home I stick them in the ground and they grow no trouble. That one, that one, I get them from the gala for the school, and polyanthus from the school too – red, purple, pink. But over here it's all from the old place – kaka beak, gladdies, gerbera, hydrangea – it's my own mother's flowers from the old place.'

'Does Uncle Max help you?'

'Useless, he don't know a kotimana from a flower. Nah, I just sit on my cushion and do what I want to do, then move along. Next day another part, or whatever I want. Well if there's digging Max can do it. He's not so old like me, only handicap, but still strong. My mother's forty-six when she have him and I'm twenty. Well it's me who bring him up all his life . . . Now dear get me a leaves from my little tree.'

Lucy picked the leaves and helped her aunt to the car. She opened the door and held the old lady as she eased her way on to the seat. She helped her get her legs in and put the shawl across her knees.

'Lovely car, dear,' Waimarie said. 'Warm, nice sheepskins.'

'Kids bought us the sheepskins not long after we got the car.'

'Who's home with you and Jimmy now?'

'Only Teina. Teina's the only one still home.'

After they'd been driving a while, Lucy said, 'We've got room Aunt, if you want us to have the girls.'

'They won't come,' said Waimarie. 'Won't even go to their own mother. Too haurangi that one. That's why I take them off her in the first place. She give them flash names and that's all. She come here wanting them last Christmas – now she sees them pretty and growing up – but they won't go. "We're stopping with Nanny," they tell her. Anyway all beer talk. She only ask for them when she's haurangi.'

'Yes, I suppose . . . Or Uncle Max. We could have him. Jimmy likes Uncle Max, those two get on like a house on fire.'

'Well it's me who bring him up all his life.'

Lucy pulled over and stopped the car.

'That's true . . . but, if ever you want . . .'

'What time they bringing Bill in?'

'Two. Leaving the undertakers at two, and should be here by ten past. Sit there I'll come round.'

Lucy helped the old lady out of the car and they moved towards the wharenui where others waited in the sun.

'I was here earlier, Aunt,' Lucy said. 'Everything's ready, house is ready. Hone, Mattie and Watson are doing the kai, and there'll be more helpers this afternoon and tonight.'

'Kei te pai,' the old woman said.

Then Waimarie stopped and said to Lucy, 'Later on dear, later on I want them to come to you, Ariana and Keriata,'

'Kei te pai, Aunt.'

'The house can be for Max, well it's me who bring him up all his life. And . . . someone can come there and live with him. Later on. Dear, I want the girls to come to you and Jimmy.'

'Kei te pai, Aunt, don't say anything more.'

Waimarie moved to greet the men at the front of the wharenui.

'You see him out,' she said to one of them.

'Tough breed,' the old man replied.

'Me too,' she said.

'The wicked stay healthy.'

Lucy assisted her up the two steps on to the verandah where those who were waiting stood to greet her.

'You're here,' someone said.

'With teeth.'

'We can get the show on the road then.'

'Where's Uncle Max?'

'Burning our house down might be.' She sat down to wait, 'You all got a warm, nice place here in the sun. Poor old Bill, ah well.'

She looked out over the marae to where the mats had been put down for the casket. The seating was ready for the family coming in and the grass had been cut and the edges trimmed. As she waited she twisted the trail of leaves into a band for her head.

When the group saw that the people were ready at the gate they helped Waimarie to her feet. Lucy put the shawl about her aunt's shoulders. The old lady moved forward to the top step and the group closed in behind her.

There was hot sun on her lifted face, sun which swathed light through her hair and sifted the circle of leaves into layers of green. And then she called their kinsman to his home, called him to the warmth, the protection of the place where he would be wept for.

The light showed the lines on her face to be deep and hard, and light spun off the gold clasps which clutched the ornaments at her ears. These ornaments hung quivering in the brightness, curving the way her jaw curved, light sculpting them against the contour of her jaw. She called the spirits of the many dead to gather along with the kinsman, so that the dead could all be wept for together.

Light mixed the muted colours of her shawl and glossed the dark clothing. And her voice lifted out, weaving amongst the sheddings of light, encompassing the kinsman and his family, bearing them forward.

The Geranium

After the kids had gone to school Marney started on the work. She did the dishes, washed the teatowels and hung them out. She wiped down the table and the bench, and the windowsill and the frame of the window. She cleaned the window and the fireplace, and took the ashpan out and emptied it where she'd been digging. She wiped the hearth with a damp cloth.

Then she put the mat outside so she could sweep and mop out. She liked the mat, which was new. Bob had come home with it the week before and she'd put it in the centre of the room where it wouldn't get marked. She thought Bob might get another mat for by the door, not a flash one, just a little rope mat to step on. She began sweeping, moving from the kitchen to the bedrooms. She was sorry the kids were all at school now, and she thought about having a job. She swept, getting into the corners with a dustpan and brush. Some of the women had kitchen jobs or did part-time cleaning, or did machining down at Hayes.

When she'd finished sweeping she got a bucket of water and a mop and mopped out. She scrubbed the back step and mopped the porch, then opened the window and door to let the breeze blow through, hoping that the floor would dry out quickly before Sandra and Joey came. She was looking forward to mid-morning when Sandra and Joey and their kids might call in on their way to the shops. Before they came she would put on her cardigan to hide her arm.

She went out into the washhouse and began rubbing the clothes that were soaking in the tub. If she had a job she'd get her a washing machine. Not a dear one, just a second-hand. She'd seen washing machines advertised in the Wanted to Sell column of the paper that came on a Wednesday. Tomorrow. At about two o'clock every Wednesday the woman came with the papers. Tomorrow there'd be another paper. And when it arrived she'd stop what she was doing and have a read, sometimes reading right up to the time the kids came home from school. But she didn't read everything on the Wednesday.

There were all sorts of things to read – stories about people of the district, or about some new building going up. A picture of their street had been in once, showing one of the Works' trucks loaded with shrubs that were being given out to each house. She liked reading about sports and the different things that people did, and there was a cooking section and sometimes a special section about gardens.

The Public Notices took up two pages and told about meetings and raffles, or where you could buy firewood or coal or an incinerator. Or you could read about garage sales and jumble sales, and where to send clothes and household goods that you didn't want. Sometimes there were notices of market days advertising produce, crafts, jumble, quick-fire raffles, white elephant, lucky dips and knick-knacks. Sometimes there were auctions with everything going cheap.

If you wanted to join a club you could read through the notices and find the one you liked, and anyone could join. The notices said things like 'Enrol Now', 'Special Welcome to New Members', 'All Welcome', 'Intending Members Welcome'. And there was one big ad that always had 'We Need You' in extra large print.

There were a lot of church notices telling the times of the services, and where you could ring for further enquiries. There were notices about where you could get advice to do with money or marriage or the law.

The schools put their notices there when they were having elections or fundraising, or when it was time for the kids to enrol. Or people could enrol at dancing school to learn ballet, tap or jazz. They could do Tae Kwan Do, aerobics, or collect spoons, just about anything. They could learn something, like swimming or ceramics or floral art.

She liked flowers. She had looked after her shrub and it was starting to grow. Sometimes she'd thought about having a few bulbs and poking them in round underneath the shrub. Or a geranium. She thought about having a geranium which could be red or pink. She liked red, but pink was all right too.

There were three pages about houses in the paper, where it told you about each house, how many bedrooms, what sort of fireplace, if there was a carpet, whether there was a garage or a double garage. Some of the houses were great for kids, some were close to shops or schools, or only a step to the railway station. Some had fabulous views. There were photos of a lot of the houses, and she liked counting the windows and looking to see if there was a chimney or two chimneys, or no chimney at all.

It was good looking at all the advertisements to do with things for the house. And there were clothes adverts about fashion frocks, fashion jerseys, fashion sweat-tops. And babyknits, fleecy and supafleece, flexiwool, polywool, wonderwool. There were pictures of nightwear and shoes and slippers, and the ads told the sizes and colours you could get. Sometimes you could get 'All Sizes, All Colours'.

Then there were the grocery and meat ads, which had the prices of everything and told you which were special and how much off, or how much for two, and there were coupons and competitions, and how to put money aside for Christmas.

And there were jobs advertised too, jobs for all sorts of tradespeople, for office workers, sales people, machinists, cleaners and kitchenhands. Sometimes people advertised for someone to mind children after school, or to do house cleaning for a few hours each week.

She liked the page where people put in what they wanted to buy or sell – like beds, bikes, lawn-mowers, pianos, washing machines, TV sets or aerials, high-chairs, freezers, fridges, pine-cones, vacuum cleaners.

But she didn't read everything on the Wednesday. She saved some of the reading for the next day, and the day after that. She always hid the paper away when she'd finished reading so that it wouldn't get put in the fire.

When she'd finished washing and rinsing the clothes, she wrung them and put as many as she could into the bucket ready to take out. She went inside for her cardigan and saw that the floor was nearly dry. If Sandra and Joey came before it had dried properly she'd put paper down, or she could mop again afterwards, just in the places where they'd walked.

The teatowels she'd put out earlier were dry, so she took them down and began pegging the clothes, returning to the washhouse every now and again to refill the bucket. There weren't enough pegs for all the washing and she had to drape the towels over the line without pegging them. She thought she might mention about the pegs.

When the women and kids came she was pleased and put some water on the stove to boil. She buttered some biscuits and put jam on some and cheese on some.

'You do this every day?' Sandra said, stepping on the papers.

'Yeh, what for?' said Joey, carrying the pushchair in so that it wouldn't make marks.

'You kids want a biscuit?' Marney asked.

'Take one and go outside,' Sandra said.

'Take two, one on top. And you come in after, I'll give you a banana.'

'They don't need a banana, tell them to get out and stay out.'

'Yes,' Joey said. 'Keep the bananas for your kids, these ones have been stuffing their faces all morning.'

She poured the tea, then they talked about the curtains some people were getting; there was a curtain bug going round and just about everyone was getting new curtains. They knew who it was taking the milk money too, and it was kids from the next street. Someone had seen them and called the cops, and that's who it was, kids from the next street. That skinny-bone one with the asthma was one of them.

Everyone was getting sick too. All the kids had runny noses and coughs. But not as bad as the one over the road from Sandra who ended up in hospital, but no wonder, spaghetti, baked beans. That's what they lived on, spaghetti, baked beans, spaghetti, baked beans.

Then they talked about some tee-shirts they were going to buy for the kids, and about the kids growing out of their clothes. They were going to sort some of the stuff out to give to someone.

Some of it was haddit and would have to be chucked out.

Then Sandra and Joey thought they'd better get going.

'Good cup of tea, Marney,' Sandra said. 'You coming?'

'Not today.'

'How come? You're always sticking home.'

'Bob does our shopping . . .'

'But a walk won't hurt.'

'Yeah, come for a stretch.'

'Well I'm a bit busy.'

'Busy my foot. What else you got?'

'Ironing . . .'

'Jesus, it can wait. Be back in an hour . . . a few minutes' walk, have a look around and home again . . .'

'And I might do a bit more . . . out the back . . .'

'Dead loss all right, why not let your old man dig? Anyway, what for? It's all rock, nothing grows.'

'I'll look after the kids if you like.'

'Fat chance, they've got money for lollies.'

'What about baby?'

'I could leave bubby. Yes, good, I'll leave her, and . . . better get going, otherwise we'll never get. You kids coming?'

'We want a banana.'

'Look . . .'

'Let them have a banana, there's plenty . . .'

'Well I don't buy bananas, they never last in our house the way they stuff their faces. In and out, in and out, wanting, asking. I go to the shop today, and just about all gone next day. But you . . . you always seem to have . . .'

'It's Bob, always bringing stuff.'

'Mmm. Not like my old man. Hers too. All they bring home is a skinful of booze, one's as bad as the other. Well look, we better . . . You leaving bubby, Joey?'

'Well . . .'

'Yes it's all right, leave her. When she wakes up I'll mash a banana, make some custard.'

'You sure?'

'Yes.'

'And sure you don't want to . . .?'

'Nah. Some other time.'

'OK then. There's a nappy in the bag, and her bottle.'

'Good, see you on the way back.'

Marney washed the cups and wiped the table down. The floor was dry and she collected up the paper and brought the mat in. She put milk into a pot to make custard for Jemmy.

By the time the women came back she'd changed and fed Jemmy, washed the nappy and hung it on the line. She'd taken Jemmy outside to play for a little while, and Jemmy had toddled about on the rough ground, laughing and pointing, and occasionally sitting down with a bump.

'She didn't cry,' Marney said. 'Not even when she first woke up.'

'She's good like that,' Joey said. 'Likes everybody. Easy to leave.'

'Here, we brought you a bit of geranium. Joey's got a bit, I've got a bit. They reckon you can grow it from a bit like that.'

'Good. Good, I was thinking about a geranium. Red too. It's just what I was thinking.'

But she was worried about the geranium, and after the women had gone she thought she might get rid of it. Then she decided to put it in a jar of water and put it on the kitchen windowsill.

After that she went out to do some more of the digging, working quickly to make up for the time she'd spent talking, or playing with Jemmy.

When the kids got home she went in and put the tea on. By then the clothes were dry and she took them in to iron.

The children had had tea and she'd almost finished the ironing when she heard the truck stop and heard Bob calling to the driver. After a while he came in and put the bag of groceries on the bench.

'So you been digging?' he said.

'Yes.'

'What else?'

'It's hard . . . quite rocky . . .'

'I said, what else?'

'The . . . the house . . .'

'What did you do this morning?'

'I got the kids off to school . . .'

'Well come on. Did they have breakfast, did they have a wash?'

'Yes. The kids got up just before you left and they had a wash. Then they got dressed while I was getting their lunches ready. I got them their breakfast . . .'

'Late, I suppose.'

'No, plenty of time. They went about quarter past.'

'And who was here?'

'No one . . .'

'I said, who was here?'

'No one. Just me. Just the kids.'

'Then what?'

'I did the dishes, then I wiped down the table, the bench, round the window, cleaned the window. Then I swept out and mopped out and . . . started on the washing . . .'

'What else?'

'I went and hung it out . . .'

'And?'

'I needed a few more pegs.'

He reached out and gripped her arm, she could feel his fingers bruising her. 'Stop changing the subject,' he said.

'I wasn't . . . I just thought . . . when you get the shopping.'

'Stop grizzling about pegs. If I want to get pegs I'll get pegs . . . What then?'

'Sandra and Joey called in.'

'What did those nosey bitches want?'

'Just called, on the way to the shops.'

'So you all went off to the shops, I suppose?'

'Not me.'

'How do I know?'

'No, not me. I looked after Jemmy while Joey . . .'

'Is that all you got to do?'

'No, but . . .'

'No but, no but. You better not be lying, that's all.

'They came and got Jemmy and . . .'

'Who's they?'

'Sandra and Joey.'

'Who else?'

'No one . . . No one else . . . Only Sandra's two kids but they ran on home. It was just Joey who came in, Sandra waited out . . .'

'So first you say Sandra and Joey, then you say just Joey. Can't you make up your mind?'

'Joey came in, Sandra waited for her.'

'I better not find out different.'

'And after that was when I did the garden. When the kids came home I started the tea. I brought the clothes in and . . . I've been ironing . . .'

'So, what else have you got to grizzle about?'

'No, I wasn't . . .'

'And what's that?'

'What's . . .?'

'That?'

'That's just a geranium.'

'Where from?'

'Sandra gave . . .'

'Sandra hasn't got geraniums.'

'She did. Sandra. She got it when she went to the shop . . .'

'Shop? What shop? I haven't seen any shop with those.'

'I mean she got it, from somewhere.'

'Changing your mind again?'

'No. It's what I meant. She got it, pinched if off someone's bush . . . or . . . spoke to someone and they gave it.'

'You don't know what you're talking about.' His grip tightened even more on her arm, he was beginning to twist.

'She said to put it . . . in water . . . and might grow.'

Then suddenly he let go and sat down at the table. So she went over to the stove, took a plate from the warming tray and began to dish up food. Her arm hurt. She piled the plate high and put it down in front of him.

'Chuck that thing out,' he said, so she took the geranium and put it into the scrap bucket. She could hear him chewimg the meat, sucking at the bones and shifting about in his chair as she waited for water to boil for the tea.

And as she waited she thought about the next day when Sandra and Joey might call in. She remembered that tomorrow was the day the woman came with the paper. There would be new stories and she wondered what they could be about. She wondered what there would be to look at in the pictures of clothes and things for the house.

When she had poured his tea she began stacking the dishes into the sink. She squirted dishwashing liquid over the plates and let the water run.

There would be the week's grocery specials to look at, telling about prices down and cut prices, and with crosses over the old prices and the new prices shown in big print. Some of the pictures of houses would be the same as for last week, but there'd be some new ones too, close to shops, great outlooks, good for kids. And there would be some new jobs but not very many.

She remembered that this was the time of the year that clubs put notices in about meetings, with special welcomes to new members and intending members. There could be new clubs with some different things for people to learn and do.

Then she thought about Wanted to Sell, Wanted to Buy, the page she liked best, where you could read about all the things people had for sale or would like to buy. Sometimes she read that page first, but sometimes she kept it until last to read. And she always read it slowly and carefully so that she wouldn't finish it too soon.

Behind her she heard him sucking his teeth and shifting his chair. She pulled the plug and watched the sink emptying, watched the water turning, heard it rushing in the drain.

The Lamp

There was a red lamp in church with a lit wick floating in oil that showed that God was home. God was everywhere but especially in church where the lamp burned. The lamp sat in a shiny gold basket that hung from a beam by three golden chains.

The playground was empty and the other kids had gone by the time Jeanie and Mereana had finished sweeping the classroom floor for Sister. Sister told them to go straight home, but they thought they would make their visit first, as they did on most afternoons after school.

Sister had instructed all the children that they should visit God in the church so that they would become holy. Visits got their sins forgiven – and all the marks and stains they had on their souls from fighting, forgetting, spitting, swearing, lying, being lazy, talking, laughing, playing with privates, bad manners, bad spelling and having bad companions could be cleaned off if you visited enough, and if you confessed. Your soul was a glowing white ball made of light that was inside your body seated at the base of your stomach. You had to keep it clean.

As well as visits you could store up prayers, genuflections, masses, offerings, blessings, communions, good thoughts and good deeds. If you had collected enough by the time you died you could get a good place in heaven, like a block of sky saved for you, and also it lessened the time that you needed to spend in purgatory getting your sins burned away.

The two girls crossed the playground, went up the church steps and into the porch. It was a little square porch and a good place to play Witchy in the Corner if there were enough of you, and if there was time.

But there were other things to do. They went first of all to shake the poorbox to see if it rattled. It did. There was something inside but it wasn't money. Jeanie slotted in a milk top she had saved, and Mereana found a leaf to put in. Then they went to finger the little books that told about sin and prayer, sacraments, saints, the rosary, families, the Trinity, the missions, commandments, catechism and the Far East. The books were full of big words and the girls tried to read some of them. Some of the books had pictures of holy people with sad faces and eyes looking up to heaven.

After that Mereana tried on a lady's coat that had been left hanging on a hook, but she looked silly. Jeanie tried it on and she looked silly too. It made them laugh.

Well it was all right to laugh in the porch as long as there were no telltales watching, but you didn't laugh in the church. They stretched and twisted their faces to stop themselves from laughing because it was time they went in. They clapped their hands over their mouths and turned their backs on each other, but that didn't work. Laughing wasn't much to do with faces and mouths, or backs. It came from inside somewhere. It came from way down in your stomach, filled up your chest, then exploded out of your face.

And it made you cry. They went over to the books again and found sad pictures of the saints and martyrs to look at, but that didn't help either. It seemed to make them laugh and cry all the more, which was something they would have to be sorry about later and confess. They went out of the porch and leaned over the stair-rail laughing and laughing until the laughter was all gone. Then they went back into the porch with their lips pressed together, and stood in the doorway that led into the church.

They peered into the gloom of the church looking out for Mr Ticklekiss with his mops and brooms. If there were other girls around, like at lunchtimes when there were lots of them, and when there was noise and shouting outside, it was quite funny when Mr Ticklekiss came sneaking up to tickle and kiss them. They'd get up and run along the kneelers and dive under the pews. Their lips would come unstuck and they'd giggle and squeal with Mr Ticklekiss coming after them. Then suddenly Mr

Ticklekiss would open a door and disappear. They'd go out later and they'd see him clearing the gutters or weeding the paths. He wouldn't look at them or speak.

But sometimes, like now, with no noise and no people, it was scary, because Mr Ticklekiss was like his mops and brooms. He had no footsteps, and he came out of the church walls or from out of the posts of the church with no noise. He was tall and spooky, and his long, pale hands flapped at the ends of his sleeves as though they had been just sewn there, the way that dolls' hands sometimes were.

Mereana and Jeanie looked into all the corners of the church. They looked at all the posts and hiding places of the church and along all the pews. There was no one – not even Bird Lady, who came every morning and afternoon on her bike with her shawl fluttering and flapping behind her. In church she would kneel in the front pew, as still as one of the statues, with her shawl pulled closely about her.

There was just the quiet, dark church with the statues looking down, and the Stations of the Cross, which were nothing but square shadows high on the walls. There was the terrible gaping loft where the choir sang for high mass on Sundays, and there was the little red glow that was the lamp, which showed that God was home.

The girls reached for the holy water, signed themselves with it and went in. They kept their lips jammed together so that no sound would escape.

They genuflected and went up to kiss the big toe of the crucified Jesus, the toe worn and shiny from being kissed thousands of times. The crucified Jesus had big square-headed nails in his hands and feet, in nail holes surrounded by pink blood. There was more pink blood on his forehead beneath the crown of thorns, and pink drops coming from the spear hole in his side. Mereana and Jeanie really felt sorry for Jesus. He gave every drop of his blood to make them good but they were bad all the same. They looked at each other with sad faces, making sure they kept their mouths shut tight.

Then they knelt to pray the 'Our Father', 'Hail Mary' and

'Glory Be'. They said acts of contrition and kept kneeling even though their knees hurt. Now that their eyes had adjusted to the light they could see the wall pictures which made up the Stations of the Cross. It really wasn't fair about poor Jesus in the garden sweating out his pink blood, then being sold, and whipped and laughed at, and having all his clothes torn away. After that he was made to carry the big cross all the way to Calvary.

But if they prayed hard enough, and did good deeds, then Jesus might think it was worth it. It was like helping him. If they could be really good then they were being like the man Simon who helped Jesus when he fell. Or they were like Veronica, who went up to Jesus and wiped his face with a towel. Then Jesus put his face on the towel like a photo. If they prayed hard, and were good, and had sore knees, and if they kept their lips shut tight and pressed the palms of their hands together, then Jesus might be able to look down and see it was worth it as he sat up there in his chair beside his father with a new crown on his head. He might smile.

Just then, while they were kneeling and praying, one of the Sisters came in carrying an unlit candle and a window pole. She put the candle down, reached up and hooked the window pole into the ring underneath the basket and pulled the lamp down.

The girls watched as she took out the red glass bowl with the light in it, then put it down on the communion rail where she would put in more of the oil and change the wick. But before she blew the flame out she lit the candle, so that while the lamp was out there was the flame of the candle to show that God was everpresent in the church. It was called perpetual light.

Then when Sister had relit the lamp she picked up the gold basket and the candle and went out. The girls knew that she would be out in the sacristy cleaning the gold basket with Brasso, rubbing to make it shine.

But just now, there was the little glowing lamp sitting on the communion rail, right down low where they could see.

They nodded to each other and stood, moving quietly along the kneeler, out of the pew and up to the rail. They stared and stared at the little flame that showed God's everpresence. They squatted, and peered up through the red glass at the dancing flame. It was difficult to keep their lips tight together.

They stood up again and Jeanie leaned over and blew, very gently, on the flame. It danced and shimmered. Mereana blew too, softly, and the wick began to sail gently in the oil, carrying its little fire.

Jeanie and Mereana looked at each other for a moment, then they both leaned over the little lamp and blew hard, together. And suddenly the flame was gone.

Gone. They grabbed hold of each other and shut their eyes, waiting for the high roof to crack and fall, waiting for the walls to come smacking down. They held on to each other, waiting, listening. God was gone, and now the Devil could come leaping down out of the choir loft and throw them in fires. They clung together for a long time in the silence, then after a while they opened their eyes. Then they ran.

They ran clattering down the aisle, through the porch, down the steps and across the playground. And Mereana, who thought she might get left behind, grabbed the back of Jeanie's tunic and yelled 'Wait!'

They ran out of the gate and down the street, with Mereana yelling 'Wait!' and Jeanie yelling 'Let go, let go!'

At the crossing they stopped, breathing hard, and they stared into each other's wide-open, round eyes. Then they ran again, across the road and along the footpath, dodging in and out amongst the shoppers until they came to the street where they both lived. They stopped there and leaned against a fence, picking grass which they held against their sides to take away stitch.

'We both did it,' Jeanie said, just to make sure.

'Yes.'

Then they sat without speaking, knowing that their souls had shrivelled inside their bodies, that they'd killed God and let the Devil loose to come grabbing them by the ankles and tossing them into everlasting fire.

They waited. After a long time they knew it was late. Lights were going on in houses.

It was *really* late and they were both going to get hidings, good hidings. For a while they talked about the hidings they were going to get. They didn't care because they deserved it. They wouldn't cry. Tomorrow, in the morning, they'd tell each other how many hits. They'd tell if they cried or didn't.

They began to run along the street that they both lived in, pushing open their gates, running along their paths.

'Count.'

'Don't forget to count.'

'And we'll tell each other.'

'In the morning.'

'We'll tell.'

'Tell.'

'Don't forget.'

'In the morning.'

'Tomorrow in the morning.'

The Wall

The old man was the only one liked our wall, or the only one said. Our wall got in the papers.

We saw the woman there with her camera, and a guy was with her having a look, writing stuff on a pad. That's good, us and our wall's going in the paper.

The day the man and the woman came was packing-up day, clearing up our rubbish, loading the gear. Only four of us and Lindsay. The others were already gone off on a new job, foot-paths down Tamihana Road somewhere. Footpaths are all right but walls are better. Well to me it's a good wall.

It took three months, and at first we didn't know what the hell. Just hacking away at the bank, mixing concrete, carting rocks. Then Lindsay got us going on it, how to put down a bit of the mix, lay one of the rocks, and keep on going like that. But not just any rock. You have to pick out a good one, the right one, the right size and a good shape to fit in with the one you just done.

We all scrapped over which rock. That one. Nah. Ha, ha, haw, haw, like that. Then try them out to see which one. A lot of times my rock was the good one, fitted in just right, ha ha ha, hee hee, get stuffed. Hee, hee, ha, ha. Haw, haw, haw. It was only easy after a while.

So our wall got started and it was pretty good, only easy, and every day there was this new bit of wall. Not just straight. Higher some places, lower some places, and got a bend in it where the road goes round.

Every morning we mucked around and had a look what we done yesterday. My rock, ha, ha. Mine, haw, haw. Stink one, slack one, ha, ha, ha, then Lindsay yells out to get on with it.

Plenty of people went past, in cars, or walking, but they never said. Drive past, have a look, keep going. Walk past, have a look, keep walking. Sometimes the kids stand around on their way home from school and have a stare, have a talk. Where you get your stones? Off the truck. But where? Don't know.

But I like the old fella best. He's the only one liked our wall.

At half past three we sent Jerryboy to get us a paper, two papers, three papers, no four.

And there was a photo of our wall all right, with a write-up about this headmaster and these parents saying how the kids couldn't see cars and buses because of our wall. Our wall was too built out.

Well too bad, at least our wall was in the paper. And us. Not looking, just loading the left-over rocks. Jerryboy's back, my hand, Pete's shoulder, and Notpeter standing up on the truck. Haw, haw. Ha, ha. Sucker. Hee hee, haw, haw, haw. I took the paper home with me at knock-off. Showed it to one or two. They didn't say much.

Anyway, this old fella came walking down the road one day. Not our side, the other side. Our wall was only about halfway then. He stopped and had a good old jack at us working. After a while he came over. He wasn't that old, just a slow walker with his breaths making a noise. Not rich.

Well, he said, and his hands were clanking round in his pockets like he had keys and ten-cent pieces, and might be a few washers and nails. And he had a big smile like he really liked us and our wall. Black old teeth. Fat stomach. Well good on you. Good on all of you and your wall. Hee, hee, hee, hee.

So Peter got up on the wall and bent his arms up and made his muscles big, pulled a strong face. Patsy swung his bum. Hee, hee, hee, squeal, squeal.

And then Notpeter, who was hosing off the footpath, stuck the hose between his legs and went yah ha, hosing all over the road. Well the old fella laughed and laughed, and squeaked and squealed with his noisy breaths. What a pisser, he shouted, hee, hee, hee. Hey, Pisser, hee, hee, hee, squeal, squeal, big funny mouth, black old teeth. Well good on all of you. Good one. Good wall. And then he went away, slow walking, big funny grin.

Well I watched out for the old fella after that, but he didn't come past again. Only cars, only kids, and people hurrying. Could be in the hospital. Could be dead. Anyway the wall's done now. Finished. We're back on footpaths again.

But if I saw the old fella, round town, down the pub, anywhere, I'd give him a yell. If he didn't remember, I'd tell him it was us made the wall. And he might say was you the pisser, and I'll say no, that's Notpeter. And he might say was you the strongman? No. The wrigglebum? No. So I might tell him I'm the one finds the good stones, ha, ha, ha, the right rocks to fit in the right place. And he'll say good one, hee, hee, squeal squeal.

Then I might say come on how about it, I'll shout you one. And he might say good on you, what are we waiting for? Then we'll go.

Electric City

After school Ani went to pay the electric city. She hoped it wouldn't make her late for work.

Harry was already home when she arrived. He'd changed his clothes and cooked chops and chips for them.

'Where've you been?' he asked

'Paying the electric city,' she said.

'Scoff this and we'll get the two-past.'

They'd almost finished eating when Pania came in. 'Did you cook any for me?'

'We're late, Parney, you get you some,' Ani said, 'and we have to leave you our dishes. Do them before Mum gets back. Make Boo help.'

'He's still playing down the road, brat.'

'And Parn, there's the old man's receipt for the power, in the drawer. You tell him.'

On the way in on the train Ani couldn't concentrate on the notes she was reading.

'Test tomorrow?' Harry asked. He had his book too, but hadn't opened it.

'Mmm. Bio. And maths Thursday.'

'We used to laugh at him, ay, when he said electric city?'

'Mmm. And I used to think what if he said it at work? People would laugh.'

'He's got this thing, about paying straight away. He thinks they'll cut the power off – the power, the phone, TV – or whatever. And he has everything counted out, this for the power, this for that, this for such and such, and such and such . . . like it's his life.'

'We were little then. Snotters. We used to really crack up.'

Then Harry said, 'I'm leaving.'

'Leaving?'

'School. I'm too old. School's for kids. I want to do something worth it.'

'Harry . . . '

'I know. Big scene. But . . . Well I skipped classes today and went down to the video shop for an interview. I reckon they'll take me. If they take me I'm quitting.'

'Look, Harry . . . '

'I've had enough. School's for kids.'

'Like me?'

'It's different. You're brainy. But me . . . I can earn heaps, work nine to nine, six days a week if I want. Old man can give up his night job. You can stay home and do homework . . . '

'But you don't have to . . . '

'Nah, I've had enough. The old man won't mind.'

'What about Mum?'

'She'll get used to it.'

The train shuttled through the cutting and they began zipping up their jackets and pushing the notes and books into their pockets.

They had three hours' work ahead of them and they hoped their boss would be there in time to open up, so they could get started early. They hoped they'd get finished in time for the two-to-nine train home.

The train scuttled out of the cutting. It was already dark. All the lights were on – row upon row of street lights winding round and winding upwards.

There were lights threaded about the harbour, and layers of light patterned the sides of the tall buildings. Beside them on the motorway the headlights of hundreds of cars beamed on to the darkening roadway.

'So it's right,' Ani said, 'It's what he means.'

'Electric City,' Harry said.

The train shuffled into the station and they looked out into the long, lit-up shelters under which commuters waited, hunching against the cold.

'Electric City,' she said. 'And you always have to pay.'

Flies

Lizzie and Mereana had just finished their jobs when Macky came with his fly.

The fly was on a short piece of cotton, which was all Macky had been able to find.

'Get some of Aunty's cotton,' he said, 'and I'll give you some of my flies.' He showed them the matchbox with the flies in it.

Lizzie went to the machine drawer, took out a reel of cotton and gave it to Macky, but she didn't want any of his half-dead flies. She and Mereana decided to get their own.

The two girls went out and looked under the shed for jars, then carried on down the track to the dunny where there were plenty of flies – like eyes, resting on the dunny walls, or down the hole singing round and round on cellophane wings.

The dunny seat and floor were still wet and stank of Jeyes, and the flies, once disturbed, buzzed and circled and zoomed. They stood still with their jars waiting for the flies to settle again. Then they tiptoed, trapping the flies with their hands, holding them lightly in their fists where they felt like live paper, and where their buzzing sounded louder and deeper.

Charlotte, Denny Boy, Ana and Erana arrived and saw that it was going to be a fly day. They went back to their own dunnies. They had better flies, they said, and knew where they could get more cotton too.

You had to be careful tying the flies. First of all you had to move the hand that covered the jar so that there was a little opening, just big enough for one fly to come out into your other hand. You had to hold the fly very carefully in your fingers so that it couldn't move its wings or legs, but you mustn't squeeze. Then someone had to tie the cotton round the neck of the fly, someone careful, so that the heads wouldn't pop off.

Well now, there they all were, holding the ends of their cottons, looking up at their crazy flies, which zigged and zagged and buzzed and dived. There they all were walking about with their flies, and sometimes the flies were little kites, sometimes little aeroplanes. Sometimes they were just silly flies making all sorts of patterns in the air, and you nearly died laughing.

But the main thing was *you* were in charge. You could lengthen the cottons to see whose fly could go highest, or you could shorten the cottons to make the flies wild and crazy, pulling and buzzing for their lives. You could buzz your fly on to someone's neck or face, which made you bust yourself with laughing. You could even let your fly go for a second if you wanted to, then jump up and grab. But the flies couldn't go anywhere you didn't want them to go. You were the boss of the flies.

After a while Denny Boy said that they could have a war and that the flies could be soldiers. Good idea. So they put themselves into teams and had partners. Someone said 'Go' and they guided the flies into each other, and the flies buzzed and fought and tangled their cottons together. Some lost wings and legs. Some died. You were allowed a new fly if your fly died, but you weren't allowed to stamp on your fly just so that you could get a better one.

At the end of the war Charlotte said that the surviving flies should be allowed to go free. Good.

'And they should have medals,' Lizzie said.

Medals, good. Charlotte snapped the head off a flower and distributed the petals. They tied the petals on to the ends of the cottons and lined up to salute while Charlotte said words.

'Here are your medals for bravery in battle and not giving up. Remember your comrades who lost wings and legs, and those who died. And lost heads. God keep you safe on your journey homeward to your loved ones. Amen.'

Amen. They let go of the cottons and watched the flies as they rose, trailing their little red medals. They waved until they thought they couldn't see them any more – or thought they could, or weren't sure. They waved just in case.

Then they turned back to the rest of the flies, dozens still crawling in the jars.

'We could send messages,' Ana said.

All right. They needed paper for messages, and pencils.

'Get the bum paper,' Macky said.

So he and Ana and Erana went to the dunny and tore the white edges off the newspapers, while Lizzie, Mereana and Charlotte went to find their school pencils.

Messages. They wrote messages in tiny writing on tiny scraps of paper that would not be too heavy for the flies to carry. They wrote Help, Save Our Socks, Save Our Sausages, Juju Lips, Tin a Cocoa, Tin a Jam, Denny Boy's got a Big One, Sip Sip Sip, Ana loves J.B., C.R. loves T.M., Bite your Bum, Macky loves Ma Fordyce.

Ma Fordyce? That made them think of writing some messages to Four-eyes Fordyce. Good idea. Fordyce has got a face like a monkey gorilla. Fordyce has got kutus. Fordyce is an old bag and a slut. Fordyce stinks, she's got a hole in her bum.

And while they were writing the messages they talked about Monday when they would all be sitting in school, and Fat Fordyce would be screwing her face up, nosing into their lunches, prodding their heads and poking their necks. And then a fly would come in, ten flies, fifty flies. Four-eyes Fordyce would be surprised and go pink. She would catch the flies and untie the messages. She would read them and go red like a tomato or a plum, or orange like a pumpkin. She would screw her mouth like a cow's bum and go round banging her strap, on desks, on seats, on anything, and she would be shouting, 'Who did this? Own up. Own up. Who did it?'

And they would all flick their eyebrows at each other, tiny, tiny flicks that only themselves could see, but they would keep their faces sad.

They finished writing and tying their messages and then

lined up with their flies facing the direction of the school. They let go their cottons and waved and saluted as the flies lifted the messages over the lemon tree, over the manuka and away.

There were still a lot of flies in their jars, so they took a piece of cotton each and tied a row of flies along each piece. They thought of using short pieces of cotton to join the rows one below another, which was a good idea. It wasn't easy, and some of the flies died, but at last the convoy was ready.

It took all of them, holding carefully, to launch it. They let go and off went the flies, crazily, pulling this way and that. It made you laugh your head off. It made you die.

There went the flies slowly rising . . . dropping . . . rising. There they went . . . up . . . drop . . . up . . . yes. Yes, they were up. Up. You ran after the flies, over the grass, through the flowerbeds, through the bushes. Go flies. Up . . . Yes. Go. There they went, higher, higher. Go flies . . . Up. Goodbye. Go to Jesus. Go to Jesus, flies. Goodbye . . . Goodbye . . . Goodbye.

Going for the Bread

After school, when her mother gave her the bread money and the bag, Mereana said that she wanted to go to the shop the long way because of girls.

'You can't go the long way,' her mother said. 'Too many cars, and too far. Go down the track. Be careful crossing the Crescent.'

'I want to go the road way,' Mereana said.

'What girls?'

'They tell me names.'

'Like what?'

'Like dirty.'

And then her mother was angry.

'Well are you? Are you dirty?'

'I don't know.'

'What do you mean, don't know. Of course you know. Course you're not dirty. We wash, don't we? Got a clean house, clean clothes?'

'Yes.'

'And don't you cry, you stop it.' Her mother was angry. 'You go down the track. And . . . if anyone says . . . anything, don't look at them. Walk straight past. You hear?'

'They might hit.'

'They won't . . . just cheeky and smart, that's all. Straight past, do what I say.'

'Yes.'

Then her mother stopped being angry. 'Bubby'll be up soon. We'll come to the top of the track to meet you. When you get to the Crescent keep on the footpath. Be careful crossing.' Then she said, 'You buy us something nice with the two pennies.'

Mereana liked the track and she could run all the way down without stopping, down the steep places holding on to the broom bushes to stop herself from sliding, over the rocky places, along the top of the bank, through the onion flowers. At the top of the bank she could climb down using the footholes that the big children had made, but today she kept to the track so that she wouldn't get dust on her clothes.

Sometimes she would stop there at the bottom of the track to watch the big children playing soccer with a tennis ball, but there was no one on the park today. She crossed the green and went up the path to where the Crescent began.

At the top of the path she stopped, looking out for the girls, but there was no one on the road, no one on the footpath. She began to hurry, not looking at gates, or people's letterboxes, or people's houses, but just looking straight ahead. No one played hopscotch on the footpath, no one skipped on the road.

It was when she rounded the corner that she knew the two girls were there. They were sitting up on the terrace looking down.

'It's her,' she heard one of the girls say, and the other girl called out a name.

Mereana didn't look at the girls, but walked quickly looking straight ahead the way her mother had told her.

Then one of the girls called, 'You're not allowed past here,' and called her the name again.

Mereana didn't look and didn't stop, and the girl said, 'We'll take your bag and throw it in the bushes if you go past here.'

She kept going, looking straight in front of her.

As she passed them the two girls came scrambling down the bank. The bigger one snatched the bag from her and ran ahead, pushing it into a hedge.

'There,' the girl said. 'Leave it there. If you get it we'll cut you with glass.'

But Mereana was going to the shop for her mother. It was her mother's bag, and the money was in the bag wrapped in a piece of paper. Anyway, the girls had run off now. They were climbing the bank again. She didn't look at them, and when she got to the hedge she pulled the bag out and walked quickly.

Then she heard the two girls scramble down the bank and

come running up behind her. They pushed her over. One of them held her while the other one cut her with glass.

Mereana's mother was frightened. She thought she should take Mereana to the doctor, but how? She couldn't take her bleeding in the bus, not while she had baby as well. She could afford a taxi one way, but it would take her ten minutes to get to the phone box and back, and she'd have to leave Mereana and Kahu by themselves while she went to ring. Also, it was baby's feed time and he was starting to yell. If she did go to the doctor, how would she get home again?

She had another look at the cut. The bleeding had almost stopped. It wasn't as deep as she'd first thought, so perhaps there was no need . . . But it could leave a scar. She didn't want her children to have scars, didn't want their father coming home from overseas and finding his children with scars.

'Babe, will I ring us a taxi and take you to the doctor?'

'No.'

'When I've fed Bubby?'

'No.'

Well all right, the cut wasn't too deep, a lot of blood though, and the scar would be just on the edge of the hair line. It would probably fade.

And another thing. She was scared about going and telling the mother what her kids had done, but she wasn't going to let them get away with it. She sat Mereana in a chair and told her to hold the facecloth against the cut.

'I'll feed Bubby,' she said. 'Then I'll help you to change your dress.'

There were bloodstains on her own clothing too, and mud on her skirt where she'd slipped on the track. She had almost dropped Kahu. The front of her blouse was wet where her milk was coming through. She undid her buttons and put the baby to her breast. He stopped crying, sucking deeply, swallowing noisily, pale milk overflowing at the corners of his mouth.

She had tried to go down the track when she'd heard

Mereana crying but she'd slipped, just letting herself slide to make sure of holding on to Kahu. Otherwise he'd be hurt too, bleeding and bruised. His father hadn't even seen him yet. She sat the baby up and he brought up wind, and she saw that he had a splash of mud in his hair.

Then she was angry again. She stood up wrapping Kahu in a rug.

'Come on, Mereana, we're going to show their mother what they did. Can you walk, Babe? Can you bring your cloth?'

'Yes.'

She moved very carefully down the track, holding Kahu in one arm while she grasped the broom stalks with her other hand. Mereana moved down behind her. When she was almost to the bottom of the track she stopped and changed Kahu to her other arm.

As they rounded the Crescent the two girls were playing up on the terrace, and when they saw Mereana coming with her mother they ran up the path and into their house. There was blood in the guttering and the glass was still there.

When the door opened Mereana's mother couldn't think what to say for a moment. Then she said, 'This is my daughter. This is what your two daughters did to her. Here's the piece of glass.'

'Get off my steps,' the woman said, 'Don't come here with your dirty daughter and your dirty lies,' and she shut the door.

Mereana and her mother went back down the path, and as they went they heard the woman yelling and running through the house. They could hear her hitting with something heavy, and there was shouting and screaming and doors banging. The two girls were getting the hiding of their lives. Their mother was in a rage, and it seemed to Mereana's mother that the woman was somehow frightened.

Kahu was beginning to cry again. He'd only had half a feed. They were all muddy and bloody, in a real mess. She was frightened too, and angry.

But there was something she knew now, something she'd made up her mind about. No one, ever again, was going to push her kids in the gutter, cut them, muddy them, make them bleed. She would never send them out alone again, not for bread, not for anything. They didn't have to have bread every day. Once a week she'd get a taxi and the three of them would go to the shops and get what they needed.

And one day the war would end.

The Urupa

When the children were almost at the top of the hill they started bagsing. Macky was the first to bags their cousin Henry but Charlotte yelled him down. He gave in, and tried for Uncle Tamati instead. But Macky couldn't have Uncle Tamati either, Macky didn't even know Uncle Tamati, only by photos. Uncle Tamati fell out of a train long before Macky came to live there. Denny Boy got Uncle Tamati.

Ana got Aunty June because Aunty June had given her a bracelet – and Erana got Bubby Pauly because Bubby Pauly was her own sister.

Lizzie got Granny Wiki and didn't need any help from Mereana or anyone.

None of them had ever known Granny Wiki, but at Aunty Connie's place there were photos of Granny Wiki with long plaits coiled about her head. They all knew that Granny Wiki used to walk out in the sea to get crayfish, bobbing down under the water while her big dress billowed up like a huge balloon on the sea. She would pop up with two crayfish in her hands and walk home. They knew Granny Wiki's favourite songs too, and had heard Aunty Connie and the others sing them plenty of times.

None of them had known Aunty Lola either, who had been brought back dead from somewhere. She had twins on top. The twins were her own newborn grandchildren. Charlotte and Denny Boy said that their Aunty Betty, Aunty Lola's daughter, had come there with her dead twins to put them on top of Aunty Lola. The twins were together in a box, Denny Boy said, smaller than a box for shoes. Well Denny Boy could be telling liars.

So Macky and Mereana would have to share Aunty Lola and the twins, or otherwise go into the old part of the urupa. They didn't like the old urupa because it was too spooky and a lot of the people there had died of a sickness that swelled them up and turned them purple. As well as that there was an old woman with wetas in her hair who came out of the ground sometimes and laughed at you, and chased you with a big stick. When you came home from the pictures in the dark you had to stop before you got to the track that led past the cemetery. You had to wait there until everyone caught up. Your legs shook and you held on to each other. Then someone shouted 'Ready Seddy Go!' and you ran and ran, yelling and crashing along the tracks through the lupins, your eyes stretching out into the dark. If you were the last one and were left behind you screamed and cried.

When you were well past you had to lie down, or bend with your head almost touching the ground, getting your breaths. And you gasped and said 'Had it, had it,' and 'Made it, made it.'

At the top of the hill they put the bottles of water and the flowers on the ground and sat down to rest.

After they'd rested a while they went over to Cousin Henry and put their ears down to listen in case Cousin Henry shouted, the way he had when he'd had his fever. Henry could call out to them and they could all dig. Or he could be trying to climb, as he did when he'd had his fever, scrambling out of bed and trying to get up the walls. They could reach their hands down and haul him up. They called and stamped on the ground. Then they listened, but there was no answer to their call, no one thumped in answer to their signals.

They listened for Bubby Pauly too, but Bubby Pauly didn't cry or talk. She could've forgotten them by now. Then they listened for the twins, but you couldn't expect . . . because the twins hadn't been born properly. They could fit inside a match-box, like two matches.

What about Aunty June then, who had come out of hospital and had her bed shifted to the front porch at Aunty Connie's? None of them had been allowed in to see Aunty June, but they could stand on boxes outside the porch and talk to her through the windows. Sometimes Aunty June would sit up against her pillows, and she'd have on one of her fine-knitted bedjackets that Aunty Myra had made, huddling over her needles like an old black spider, looping the wool up over her spider-leg fingers and letting the web of knitting heap into the hollow of skirt slung between her knees.

Aunty June was so pretty with her shiny eyes, her bright lips and cheeks, her long black hair spread on the pillow.

'Don't fight over the windows,' she'd say. 'Or I'll go back to sleep.'

So then they'd just have to let Charlotte and Denny Boy have the best windows and the best boxes, while the rest of them got wherever they could.

Then Aunty June would make them sing. 'Sing or I'll go back to sleep,' she'd say. 'Sing "Blue Smoke". Sing "Red Sails in the Sunset".' Which was as though everything was colours, floating and drifting.

So they would sing 'Blue Smoke' and 'Red Sails', and sometimes Aunty June would join in, in a high lovely voice. After that they would sing their school songs, or some of the songs from the Lifebuoy Hit Parade that Charlotte and Ana had copied into an old exercise book.

After a while Aunty Connie would come in with soup and Aunty June would say, 'Yum yum, pig's bum.' Aunty Connie would fix the pillows and put the tray down, and Aunty June's little wrist and hand reaching from the webby sleeve of the bed-jacket to take up the spoon was just like a little spoon itself.

Aunty Connie would shoo them all away, and they'd jump down from the boxes and run before they were given jobs to do.

Then one day the ambulance came for Aunty June so they all went to say goodbye. They weren't allowed to go close and could only wave. Aunty Connie was holding a towel to Aunty June's mouth. Aunty June's fingers were out of the blanket wriggling, waving a little goodbye to them. The ambulance was white with two little crosses, like little red sails, one at each side.

Well they listened for Aunty June, but they didn't expect . . . because she'd already waved. They listened for Uncle Tamati too, but how could he? He'd been smashed to bits, all in pieces on the railway track.

And anyway it was time to get on with it. Charlotte and Ana began to divide up the flowers. Charlotte needed dahlias and asters for Cousin Henry because she reckoned he liked purple and red, and he would want green leaves and yellow snapdragons as well. Denny Boy needed dahlias too, and snapdragons and some green stuff. Ana wanted the stocks, just the pink and white, but she thought she might as well have the purple too, and some green leaves. It wasn't fair if Charlotte and Denny Boy had all the green. Charlotte told Denny Boy to give some of his leaves to Ana. Erana wanted one of everything, except marigolds because they'd gone to sleep. And it wasn't fair because Charlotte and Denny Boy had all the asters. Charlotte gave her one. All the dahlias too. Denny Boy gave her one. Lizzie took the remainder of the snapdragons, and there were marigolds left for Macky and Mereana. They could have the whole lot.

So then they all went to their different places and threw away all the brown stalks of flowers that had been there since their previous visit. They swished the green water that remained in the bottom of the jars with a stick, tipped it out, then refilled the jars with water from the bottles they'd brought with them. They began arranging the flowers.

But Macky had the sulks, and he was sitting in the grass beside Aunty Lola's stupid grave. His lips were pinched together, and every now and again Mereana could hear long breaths coming out of his nose. He was pulling the petals off the stupid marigolds. Their bottle had toppled over and the stupid water was pouring out all over the place.

Mereana watched him for a while. She was angry with Lizzie who was a pig, a dog and a rat. There were a few weeds on Aunty Lola's grave so she pulled them out. Then after a while she began picking up all the marigold petals that Macky had let fall everywhere, and began scattering them over the grave.

She started at the top where Aunty Lola's face was, and worked down. Macky saw what she was doing. He watched for a while, peeping through his eyelashes.

Then he began to help, because it looked good, and it was a good idea. Yes. It was much better than banging a stupid jar at the top, a stupid jar in the middle, and a stupid jar at the bottom and bunging flowers in them – as though you were punching someone in the face and in the stomach, and booting their legs.

They worked down over where Aunty Lola's chest was, over the middle and the box of twins, right down to her feet. It took a long time. Then they climbed down the bank to where there were taupata bushes growing and picked bunches of leaves. They placed the leaves all round the edges of the grave, making a border of green. It looked beautiful. It was a good idea.

The others finished and walked round looking, talking about what they'd all done, but Mereana and Macky didn't join them. Instead, they sat down where they were and blew noises through the folded taupata leaves. They could do taxi horns, quacking ducks and seagull noises, as well as a variety of farts.

When the others came to see what they'd done they didn't look up. They kept on blowing through the leaves and only looked at Charlotte and the others through their eyelashes.

Well Charlotte was wild. She didn't say anything but she was wild all right. She stamped off down the hill. Denny Boy said 'Smartfarts', and went off after Charlotte. They heard him calling, 'Smartfarts, smartfellas, fartsmellers,' as he went.

The others stood for a moment or two looking, but they were all wild too, except for Lizzie. Lizzie danced and coughed and said, 'Gee, it's a good idea, a real good idea. It's lovely the way you've done . . . it's like a birthday. And . . . I reckon they like it. See, Ana, Erana.' But Ana and Erana had gone off after Charlotte. They were wild.

Macky and Mereana sat and explained to Lizzie how they'd taken the petals off the flowers and started sprinkling them at the top, down over the chest, twins, legs, feet – and then made a frame right round with taupata leaves. Good idea. Lizzie reckoned Aunty Lola liked it.

It was time to go. They picked up their bottles and began to hurry downhill. From halfway down they could see the others standing in the sea washing the bottles and washing their hands. So they stopped running and dawdled a little, giving them time to finish their wash. Because Charlotte would be still wild and she'd push them in the sea. Denny Boy might ankle-tap. Then they'd get a hiding from Aunty Connie for having wet clothes.

They waited until they saw the others making their way back up the beach and through the lupins, then they went down to the sea to wash.

Bloody cold too. Just as well they hadn't let Charlotte throw them in. Cold, and they were hungry as well. They began to run, up over the beach and through the lupins.

But they'd forgotten that the others might booby-trap them. Charlotte, Denny Boy, Ana and Erana had tied the lower branches of the lupins together across the skinny tracks, and the next minute Mereana, Macky and Lizzie were tripping, flying, falling on their faces, and the bottles were spinning away into the bushes. They could hear Charlotte and the others laughing in the lupin tunnels.

Anyway it was nothing. Macky and Mereana didn't care because it just proved how good their idea was. Lizzie didn't care either, and she was going to do that idea next time. She reckoned Aunty and the twins liked it.

They got up and tidied their clothes, found their bottles and went running. They were cold. They wanted a feed. They wondered what sort of a mood Aunty Connie was in.

Butterflies

The grandmother plaited her granddaughter's hair and then she said, 'Get your lunch. Put it in your bag. Get your apple. You come straight back after school, straight home here. Listen to the teacher,' she said. 'Do what she say.'

Her grandfather was out on the step. He walked down the path with her and out on to the footpath. He said to a neighbour, 'Our granddaughter goes to school. She lives with us now.'

'She's fine,' the neighbour said. 'She's terrific with her two plaits in her hair.'

'And clever,' the grandfather said. 'Writes every day in her book.'

'She's fine,' the neighbour said.

The grandfather waited with his granddaughter by the crossing and then he said, 'Go to school. Listen to the teacher. Do what she say.'

When the granddaughter came home from school her grandfather was hoeing round the cabbages. Her grandmother was picking beans. They stopped their work.

'You bring your book home?' the grandmother asked.

'Yes.'

'You write your story?'

'Yes.'

'What's your story?'

'About the butterflies.'

'Get your book, then. Read your story.'

The granddaughter took her book from her schoolbag and opened it.

'I killed all the butterflies,' she read. 'This is me and this is all the butterflies.'

'And your teacher like your story, did she?'

'I don't know.'

'What your teacher say?'

'She said butterflies are beautiful creatures. They hatch out and fly in the sun. The butterflies visit all the pretty flowers, she said. They lay their eggs and then they die. You don't kill butterflies, that's what she said.'

The grandmother and grandfather were quiet for a long time, and their granddaughter, holding the book, stood quite still in the warm garden.

'Because you see,' the grandfather said, 'your teacher, she buy all her cabbages from the supermarket and that's why.'

The Hills

I like it when I get to the top of the road and I look out and see the mist down over the hills. It's like a wrapped parcel and you know there's something good inside.

And I like being funny. When someone says something I like to have something funny to say back, because I like people to laugh, and I like laughing too. A funny man, that's me.

'Man' might not be quite the right word – but 'boy' isn't right either. 'Boy' means little kid, 'boy' means dirty with a filthy mind. It means 'smart-arse'. A 'boy' is a servant and a slave.

Well I've been grubby and smart all right but never a servant or a slave. Mum bossing me and getting me to mow grass and mop floors doesn't make me a slave or a servant. That's just something for me to moan about because I don't like doing my share. Anyway, I'm not a slave or a servant. I'm just myself. One day I'll call myself a man, and I won't just be an old 'boy' like my father.

He's gone. I've got an uncle that I really like, Mum's brother, and he's funny too. Jokes don't stop him being a man.

Some teachers don't like my jokes and they think I'm a pain, but I get on all right with a few. Once when I was in the third form I drew a neat moustache on myself. I got told off and had to go and have a wash, and I got picked on by that teacher all the time after that.

When I was in the fifth I grew a real moustache and trimmed it up, and I had about six hairs of a beard as well. Well my form teacher got screwed up about it and ordered it all off. 'The mower's broken down,' I said, and I got into a heap of trouble. Anyhow I think someone must have stuck up for me somewhere along the line. I got moved to another form class and nothing more was said about my whiskers.

They're not sharp hills, or pointy. They're bums and boobs, with cracks and splits. They're fat and folding. I like it when the wrapping comes off.

One day I wore a big long coat to school. It was an old coat but hadn't been worn much. It was just a coat that my old man had left behind, the type of coat that a lot of men wore then. Gaberdine, my mother said. She said I looked like a drongo.

The first thing the coat made me feel like doing was marching. I don't know why, because it wasn't like an army coat at all. It was big for me and down to my shins. I marched along the street and when I saw Wasi and Georgina I stopped and saluted and they fell in behind. Good on them. Off we marched for a while, until Wasi started talking about something interesting. We stopped acting up and strolled along the way we usually did.

Then when I got to school I thought I could be a flasher. So at each change of class I walked last into the room and went 'Zoonk!' I didn't flash anything of course, except for grey shirt, grey jersey and a pair of baggy cords. Some laughed and some didn't. One of the teachers grinned and yelled out 'Police!', and the whole class cracked up. I liked that. I had a good laugh too. Sometimes you just need a change from grey shirt, grey jersey, pair of baggy cords.

When the mist comes down to cover the hills I don't think grey. I think of parcels and coloured wrapping, and clothes and tits and bums. Then I have a good laugh at myself and think that I'm only a boy after all. I don't mean a servant or a slave or a smart brat. I just mean 'boy' in a different, youngish way.

Then something can happen to you that's too much for a boy. You can't be a boy any more afterwards. And when it's gone for good, and you're sure it's gone you can feel sorry. It wasn't you that did it or wanted it. It was something done to you.

You get used to the police, stopping, searching, hassling you around. They say something smart and you say something smart back. But you know you shouldn't get too smart. You have to hold back. You know they don't like you to be clever because it makes them scared. So you let them mouth off and you have to bite your tongue, which isn't easy for someone like me with jokes on his lip all the time. But after they've gone you can have a bit of a laugh – name please where are you going where've you been do you know so and so where do you live whose shoes you got on up against the car search search.

Mum doesn't like me drinking. She says there's nothing wrong with the old man, only drinking. He's all right she reckons, kind, tidy, just useless and a drunk, and she's glad he's gone. We get on better without him, she says. But anyway my mates and I enjoy drinking and parties, and I tell Mum she shouldn't worry about me.

When school finished last year, me, Wasi, Georgina, Steven, Louanna, and Georgie's brother and a few others went to the pub to celebrate. Louanna and Steve weren't coming back to school. I thought I might leave too but hadn't made up my mind. Georgie's brother was the only one old enough to be in the pub. We didn't have much money but Lou and Steve had enough to shout a couple of rounds. It was good. We were having a good time.

Then Steve went out to the toilet and didn't come back. Wasi went to have a look, and when he came back he said that the cops were outside talking to Steve.

Lou and Wasi and I went out to have a look, and on the way we were cracking jokes about Steve leaving school and going straight to Rock College. Ha, ha. There was a cop car outside with two cops in it but no Steven.

We looked round but couldn't see him, had another look in the toilets and he wasn't there, so we went back outside.

I went over to the car and looked in the window. I knew Steven wasn't in the car but I said, 'Have you got our mate Steven in there?' Then I was slammed in the head with the door, jerked to my feet with my arm up behind, and hung over the bonnet of the car. They went down and through my pockets and one of them said, 'Take him in.'

'You can't do that. What for?' That was Louanna yelling at them.

'Get home, girlie,' one of them said. He threw me in the car and started up.

Louanna started booting the car and shouting, 'What about me, look what I'm doing.'

'Shove off,' one of them said, and away we went.

'What for?' I said. I'd got over the bang on the face by then, and just thought that it was the same game, only rougher than usual. They'd drop me off any minute as long as I didn't get too smart.

'Shut your black face,' one of them said. 'You'll know soon enough.'

Well some are polite and some aren't, even though they are mostly all playing the same game.

'Abusive language,' the other one said, 'and resisting arrest.'

I was just drunk enough to say, 'I thought it was for under-age drinking.'

'That too,' they said.

And then I was just drunk enough to say that anyway, they were the ones being abusive telling me to shut my black face.

'Why?' the same one said. 'You've got a black face, haven't you? You're a black, aren't you?'

Well he had me there. If I pointed out that I was brown it was like denying blackness, like saying you're halfway to white.

'It's not an offence, is it?' I asked.

'No offence me saying what you are then, is it?' the smart one said.

I could see they weren't going to let me out of the car. Sometimes the game can be quite amusing, something for a laugh later, but I was slacked off with their game this time.

At the station I was charged and asked a whole lot of questions. I just answered the questions and tried to point out that I wasn't drinking when they saw me, I wasn't in the pub when they saw me. I was sober by then. Anyhow the sooner I got out the better, I thought, so I decided I should keep my mouth shut.

The smart one went out for a minute or two then came back in. He held the door open and jerked his head, so I followed him through into another room where I was grabbed and searched again. Then suddenly I was thrown across a bench, my trousers were pulled down and I was searched up the behind.

That's what I meant when I said something can happen, and you can't be what you were after that. I said 'searched' but

I didn't know at the time that what they were doing was part of a search. I thought I was being raped. I didn't know then – or if I'd heard of it I'd forgotten – that people sometimes hid things up there.

Afterwards I remember feeling sick, and going out and my mates being out there waiting, and us all going to Georgie and her brother's place. I remember crying. They all thought I'd been beaten up and I didn't tell them any different.

They wanted to ring my mother but I said no. I didn't want her to know. Steve and Lou were staring at me. I don't know what I looked like.

'What do you want? What will we do?' Louanna asked.

'I want to have a bath,' I said. 'I want to go to sleep.'

I stayed in the bath a long time, and when I got into bed I stayed awake a long time.

In the morning Georgie said, 'We rang your Mum just to tell her you were staying the night.' She waited a while. And then she said, 'You sore?' So I told them what happened.

But I didn't tell Mum when I got home. I told her I'd been caught under age in the pub and had to go to court. She banged me on the arm and then she cried.

Later that day I went outside and walked up the street, and when I got to the top of the road I wouldn't look out at the hills. The hills could've been clear, or the mist could've been down or it could've been just lifting off. I turned and went back home. I remember wondering if I would ever look there again.

Fishing

While the others were out getting paua and kina, Ria fished. She'd picked ngakihi off the sea rocks, then taken the line and bait to a place where there was weed. The waves were green there – not heavy, and not breaking until right on shore. On shore they broke, tracking up over the stones.

She thumbed ngakihi out of their shells and baited the hooks, then unwound some of the line and walked to the edge of the water, whirling the traces. She cast, and the line shot out, dropping close to the weed.

From where she sat she could see the others, some out diving off the dinghy to pick kina off the sea bed, others snorkelling about amongst the rocks getting paua. That was the way the younger ones liked to do things, yet she knew if they'd waited until the tide was down they could've walked out and got all the paua they needed, in water that was just knee deep.

Further out past the divers, the children were jumping off Chicken Rock, struggling in the breaking waves and climbing up again. In the shallow water younger children were pushing a log about, and babies paddled and played, watched by mothers who really wanted to be getting kina and paua, or out jumping off Chicken Rock. If she'd stayed there with them she would've watched the kids and given her nieces a break. But today she'd decided to go off on her own and fish.

There were a few tugs on her line and then the biting stopped. She began to pull in, knowing that the bait would be gone, bringing the line in swiftly so the sinker wouldn't snag. Ngakihi was soft bait but would have to do until the water was shallow enough for her to get paua. She baited up and cast the line again – not straight, not far, but the spot was worth a try.

Looking back she could see the old man sitting under the big umbrella. He would be watching, thinking about the place, thinking about how he knew the shape of the sea bed right there. She knew he would like to have told someone about when the crayfish were thick, about when you could, at this time of the year, have looked down from the hills and seen the large red mass moving shoreward, which was crayfish coming in. She would have listened to him tell about how they'd pulled the weed aside with long-handled spears to find the crayfish that had backed themselves into narrow cracks in the rocks. The old man liked the umbrella.

Out on Chicken Rock the children were facing out to sea, waving. There was the sound of a motor, and then a boat came into sight and began weaving its way in. She couldn't see clearly but knew it would be her cousin May, with her husband and their family, coming to catch what could be the last good tide of the summer. The boat stopped close to shore and the children got out, then it rode out again to where May and Maru would set their nets.

The fish were biting all right, but she wasn't hooking them. She pulled in and baited up again.

Now the kids out on the rock were calling, looking shoreward this time. They would be tired by now, wanting someone to bring the dinghy out to get them. She watched as someone rowed out and nosed the boat up against the big rock. The children climbed down to be taken ashore, too exhausted and too hungry to swim for it. They were soon back on shore, running everywhere picking up sticks. They wouldn't be given bread until the wood had been gathered. Not long after that she saw smoke rising against the backdrop of cliffs. The divers were wading in with full bags.

At low tide she went to look for paua. There were several there on the stones and she collected three. She washed and shelled the smallest one, intending to eat it. Then she decided she wouldn't eat until she had caught her fish. She wouldn't eat, and she wouldn't go back to drink tea. Knowing that her line would snag in such shallow water, she lay down, sheltering where the stones had piled, and waited for the tide to flow again.

For some time there was little activity in the incoming tide. Then suddenly the fish were there again, biting and pulling, and she knew it was just a matter of time.

It was colder now but the kids were back in the water again – the mothers too, getting their chance at last. Cassie was helping the old man up to the car, wanting to get him home before the cold set in. The old man liked being able to come there by car.

By the time she caught her fish it was late afternoon. It was a small fish, but she was satisfied. All she'd hoped for was to catch one fish on this, the last good day of summer. She took it down to the water's edge where she cleaned and scaled it.

Then she knew there was something else for her to do, because how could you be really sure of coming there again next summer? And why should you come if you didn't let the place know you? It wasn't enough just to hold at the end of a line. The mothers were right about needing to go beyond the shore.

She walked out into the half-tide and let herself gradually into the water. She squatted for a while with her skirt floating up about her, then she pushed forward and down, pulling herself along the stony sea bed for as long as her breath lasted. When she came to the larger rocks where the weed grew thickly, she stood and pushed her way through. Once in the clear water again she lay on her back, letting herself go the way the water moved her. It was a familiar place, and she knew she could lie there like that quite safely.

She lay there for a long time watching the sky redden as the sun went down.

Back on shore she picked up her line and the little fish, and walked quickly back to where the others were sitting round the fire, or getting ready to go for the nets.

They were amused at her one little fish, that it had taken her most of the day to catch. She knew they were wondering why she would spend all day on her own, without food, then come back wet and cold with just one little fish, especially when she knew there would be plenty of fish once the nets were brought in.

But it was her cousin May who said to her, as though they were picking up a conversation that could have begun years before, 'Because if you don't, it's like you won't any more. It's like if you sit under the umbrella once, then that's it. You have

to still know, and you have to do enough . . . to carry you over.
You have to be in there because you don't want to be just waiting
by the edge.'

Kahawai

All right then. One morning I got up late and hurried to the kitchen. He was up before me and would have the jug boiling, the pan plugged in, the bread popped down, I thought.

Instead he was in the front room looking out.

Because the gulls had gathered out at sea, under cloud, and were chasing, calling, falling to the water. Up, chase, drop. Screaming. There's fish, he said. It brought juices. Kahawai, beating green and silver through purple water, herding the herrings which excited the gulls, which excited me . . .

Could we . . .?

Be sick?

We could.

Have we got . . .?

Bait?

We have.

Have we got two-stroke?

No.

Get breakfast, get changed, get two-stroke.

Have we got spinners?

No. Someone borrowed.

Don't need spinners. Can trawl the heads of soldiers.

Then the others came in.

Well . . . what? Have yous got a holiday or something? Or what?

We're sick . . .

Of work.

And the fish are out there, nose to tail.

Yes, we heard.

The birds.

Saw splashes. But . . .

It's only us who don't go. Sometimes. Or don't get up. Right? Because of hangovers, or laziness, or going somewhere else. Or from not being back from somewhere. Only us have

77

sickies. Right? But anyway . . . Good. Good on yous. Kahawai,
yum. Make some bread too. Yahoo.

Lines, bait, knife, hooks, sinkers, jerseys, towel, apples, can of
two-stroke, putt-putt motor, rowlocks, oars. Push the dinghy out
and sidle out past the weed.

He winds the rope and pulls, tries again and then we're
away putt-putting out over the navy blue, under cloud, stopping for a while to remove the sinkers from the lines and to bait
the hooks with the heads of soldier fish.

Then away again to where the gulls swarm above the
swarming kahawai that herd the swarming herrings. But he and
I are not a swarm, we are only two of us. One fish each will do.

Then we are in the middle of it, the darting, leaping little
fish crack open the dark water, leap and splash, the gull's eye
singling out one, the eye of the kahawai on another. Gulls
swooping, following, rising, diving, rising, swallowing, turning,
following. And the kahawai zigging, zagging, leaping, shooting
through the water, beating silver on the surface of it. Hundreds.
But for us two will do.

We trawl our long lines with the putt-putt on slow, putt-
putting through chaotic water under the screeching canopy.

Of birds. One of them is eyeing the bait, the head of the
soldier, and is following. I stand spread-legged and wave one
arm. No. Go. Silly bird. It's dead meat, hooked. Krazy Karoro.

Krazy Kahawai too, for that matter. And Krazy Kataha.
K.K.K. And what about Krazy Kouple in a boat? K.K.K. and
K.K. I wave. Shout. Go, Karoro, go. So Karoro drops back, but
still follows, still wants.

And then, Got it, he says. So I stop waving, stop shouting,
plonk myself down. He switches the motor off so that he can
pull in . . . number one. Pulling . . .

What have we here?
One little kahawai, my teacher dear.
Kahawai, Kahawai, nicky nicky nacky noo,

> *That's what they taught me*
> *When I went to . . .*

Pulling . . . Pulling in over the side . . .

> *Flip flop she flied,*
> *Flip flop she flied,*
> *Flip flop she flied,*
> *She went up to heaven and flip flop she flied*
> *Flip flop she fliedy flied flied . . .*

Krazy Kahawai flapping, slapping the tin boards of the boat, bouncing in the wet sack on the tin bottom of the boat. I pull in too so that my line won't tangle in the motor while we start up again.

Off. Putt-putting full out to catch up with Karoro again. They have moved further out now, dinning and diving. We trail the heads of soldiers, turning to run with the fish . . .

> *Kahawai, Kataha, nicky nicky nacky noo,*
> *That's what they taught me . . .*
> *Hat on one side what have we here?*
> *One little chin chopper, my teacher dear.*
> *Chin chopper, snot catcher, eye basher, sweaty boxer,*
> *   nicky nacky noo*
> *That's what they taught me when . . .*

Karoro. Again. Eyeing, swooping. I stand, wave, shout. Not for you. Shoo. Wave and shout. Go. Blow. Karoro backs off, then moves up again. I pick up an apple, throw it, and Karoro turns, circles, returns. Krazy Kamikaze Karoro. I pick up the towel, swing it, and Karoro, nervous, drops back, still wanting, still turning the eye.

But then, is beaten to the bait by Kahawai. Number two. Got it. He switches off and I sit down pulling in swiftly . . .

> *One little kahawai my teacher dear,*

Kahawai, Kahawai, nicky nicky nacky noo,
That's what they taught me when . . .
Kahawai, Kahawai, nicky nicky nacky noo,
That's what they . . .
What have we here?
One great big kahawai my teacher dear,
Kahawai, Karoro, Kataha, Krazy Kouple, nicky nicky
* nacky noo,*
That's what they taught me . . .

Bring it in over the side, hand into the gills, push the hook. Look
Karoro, hook, turn your eye. Not meant, not bent for a feath-
ered throat. Open the bag and . . .

Flip flop she flied,
Flip flop she flied,
Flip flop she flied,
She went up to heaven and flip flop she flied
Flip flop she fliedy flied flied.

And now, the gulls, the fish have moved out again, too far for
a tin boat and a putt-putt on a cold day. It's Kold, and two will
do. One flick and we're moving again, turning, the Krazy
Kouple. Kold. Heading home.

As we come to the weed in the shallow water we switch
off, lifting the motor, and row in swiftly. Kold. We step out,
ahh, into water, kold hands gripping the sides of the boat. Can
we lift it? We can, rushing it up over the stones. Rest, then again.
Again, blue knuckled. And lift. Can we? On to the trailer? We
can.

Then back to the edge we go with the two fish, scraping
fast, because it's kold. The scales leap. We slit the white bellies,
pulling the insides out, flinging. Kum Karoro. They come, dance
on the surface of the sea, snatch the innards and fly up gulping.
We wash the fish and the water runs red-salt-blood. We hurry
with the trailer, home, to be dry and warm.

When it is time I put bread in the oven. He cuts up fish, puts it in the big pot with a good fist of salt, watches so that it won't boil fast. We scrub and slice vegetables and put them on to cook.

Then the others come, lifting the lids of the pots. Did yous? Yous did.

Opening the oven door.

Did yous? Yous did. Yum.

When it is time we lift the fish carefully into bowls and strain the water into a jug. We break up the bread on the board and heap the vegetables on to dishes.

Then we sit down to celebrate.

Hospital

There's something being hauled up from inside her – up and out of her throat – something sharp and cutting, and live. She is puffed up and big – this one of her. The other one of her is small, sitting cross-legged on air, still and serene, watching.

It's fish, bunches of tarakihi with splayed fins, tearing the insides of her, tearing her throat, ripping her stretched mouth – and then falling in heaps about this swollen, inert one of her, pale, bloodied and flopping. She can smell the sweet, green smell of live fish. There are voices and noise.

The other one of her, sitting unmoving in the shadows, is telling her something – not about fish, fins, falling, bleeding or noise, but about the pain – warning her not to let it go. Above all the clamour and the fish stink, there is the precious, grinding pain that she mustn't let go – must keep . . . keep . . . keep . . . The other one of her, sitting still in the shadows, is warning her, so that in the sudden stillness she won't let herself slide . . . or shift . . . or drift . . .

Without the sounds, without the movement, there's only the solid pain to hold.

Taking hold. It of her. Her of it. And then slipping. She slipping. It slipping . . . Out through her feet? No. The other one of her, sitting straight-backed and unmoving is telling her to reach . . . reach . . . threatening that if she doesn't, then someone else will get her pain, as a legacy. Someone else will have, as inheritance, what only you should . . . you should . . . you should . . .

'Who?'

'Your daughter.'

'No. I have it, have it now, safe, and keep it to my bloated, bloodied, groaning, fish-woman self. Don't speak . . . of daughters. No more slip, slide. No slipping, sliding. Just hold, hold, holding . . . until it is . . .

Time.

Shouting.

A name.

Her name.

Faces.

She knows one of . . .

Voices.

She knows one . . .

'How . . . feeling? Feeling? How . . . feeling?'

Sore. She knows she hasn't said it.

'Feeling?'

She finds breath, pushes it out. 'Sore,' but it is only a whisper.

'Yes, I'll bet. Anyway, good enough . . . let you . . .'

Rest.

And she's looking down on a bare world where naked people crawl on a dry earth searching . . . for kai.

. But there is no kai. It's a world of sand, and the figures crawl like insects over its surface, thin-limbed, large-eyed, dry, flaky.

'Looking down from where?' she calls to the other one of her.

'From where you are.'

'Don't want . . .'

'But anyway, there it is. There they are.'

'Don't want . . .'

'Otherwise who else? Who will see? Who will know?'

'Dreaming.'

'Not dreaming.'

'Dreaming.'

'Not dreaming.'

Waking.

There are patches of light, smudges of dark, circling. Green counterpane and two arms. Hers. Her two arms on a green counterpane. A tube going upwards. Blood.

'Warm enough?'

'Yes.' It is only a breath.

'Lost your voice, hmmm?'

'Blood.'

'And look, flowers. Nice, ay?'

But she knows there's no place for flowers.

Or fish. No place for the pop-eyed tarakihi, hands pulling, hooks, lines, seaweed, sharp fins. No seas or rivers. Only . . . insect people with long hands, and feet that are hand-like. They crawl with their noses close to the ground. They cry into the ground, long fingers scratching at the earth, long toes spread, finger-like, patterning the sand.

'Don't want to see.'

'Want or not, there they are. Otherwise who?'

'Dreaming.'

'No. Not dreaming.'

'Dreaming.'

'Not dreaming.'

Awake.

Voices.

Faces.

'. . . nice wash . . . feeling now?'

'Scared.' Has she said it? Her two arms on a green counter-pane. A tube going upwards.

'Water.'

'Fluids, to keep you going. Nice flowers, ay?'

But she knows there's no place for flowers. No seas, no rivers, only . . .

'Burning.'

'Sore I bet . . . But you'll feel a bit better tomorrow. We'll take the drip off later, and we'll shift you down to a ward room in the morning.'

She's on a trolley, in a corridor. Wheels click over the linoleum, fast, past windows . . . windows . . . windows . . . Wheels, windows, wheels, windows – like in a tunnel, in a train.

The wheels slow down, they stop by glass doors. She's making way for a wheelchair which has been tilted on to its back wheels. They are wheeling in . . . a pig?

There was one in a barrow, trundled through the streets,

covered with apples. A prize. Only two ears and the snout with its two great snout-holes showing.

No. Not a pig. It's a woman. Her neck, crusted with dry blood, is arched back over a pillow, and her stretched nostrils are packed up with cotton.

'Now a cup of tea, love? Sit you up a bit. Mr Siers is coming soon. Better without those drips?'

'Yes.'

'No voice yet, hmmm? No water passed either. Well, drink up plenty – for the waterworks, get the plumbing going. We'll sit you out on a chair later, on a pan, see if that works. Nice carnations, ay?'

But the flowers are shocking and wrong-coloured – shocking red, shocking pink and shocking shiny gold. The stalks are bright, lime green. For a moment a woman stands by the door and the patterns on her dressing gown move away from the gown itself, shimmering . . . or else there is a trick of light. If she asks about the flowers – do they brighten, darken, do they shift and change, or about sharp fish, or the insect-shadow-people that move over the surface of the turning sand-bone world – will her questions come out wrong-coloured too? Will she yell instead, scream? She slides down off the pillows thinking about what she can safely say. She can say, 'Yes,' or 'No,' or 'No voice.' Open your eyes.

'A bit better today?'

'Yes.'

'What's happened to your voice?'

'No voice.'

'Well, don't rush it.'

Sister lifts the covers back, opens the gown, folds it away from the dressings and the surgeon touches gently about the bandages.

'What about the waterworks?'

'No.'

'No? We'll try her on some Mist. Pot. Cit., Sister, that should help. A bit sore round here?' He touches gently.

'Yes.'

'Lift the dressings a little? Yes, it's fine.' Looking down, thoughtful, kind. 'Eating?'

'Not yet, Mr Siers, but we'll see what we can tempt her with at lunch. And we'll get her moved over by the window.'

'Good, I'll look in again tonight.'

'Drink up as much as you can. See. Big jugful, drink the whole lot, that should do the trick. It's nice.'

Yes. It is nice. Lemony and cold, with a faint fizz. If it didn't work, what happened? Did you swell up and pop, like a frog?

'Nurse.'

'What is it, love?'

'Can you shift the flowers?'

'To?'

'The shelf in the corner.'

'You won't see . . .' Nurse frowns, but she takes the vases, lifts them onto the shelf.

'Is that OK?'

'Thanks.'

She can hear the trolleys rumbling down the passage bringing midday meals.

'Now, dear, they're bringing roast beef and vegetables,' Sister says. 'Is that all right? Or would you like poached eggs, a bit of pie?'

'Just the vegetables, Sister, thanks.'

'Good, and some gravy?'

'Yes please.'

'Good. Got your appetite back now, have you? And pudding? Fruit and rice, and I'll tell Nurse to put some cream on. Do you like cream?'

'Yes, thanks.'

'Good, love. I'll pop back and see how you're getting on.'

The dinner nurse comes in, beaming, with a tray.

'Here you are.'

Salt and pepper in glass shakers, and cutlery wrapped in a napkin. On the plate there is a ball of mashed potato which is pale and metallic-looking, a ball of red pumpkin, a spoon of emerald peas and a mound of navy blue silverbeet. There's a topping of reddish gravy.

She could ask what has happened to colours, or what has happened to her. Instead she asks the nurse to put the tray on the locker. The nurse looks unhappy.

'Would you like something else instead? Sister said . . .' So she relents. 'Leave it, Nurse, I'll try.'

'Good. Pud's coming. Enjoy your dinner.' Away beaming.

She puts a forkful of the potato to her mouth, swallows, and eats two of the peas. Then she leans back on the pillows. In a minute she'll have a mouthful of the drink, then try again. Someone coming.

'Not hungry today?' It's the pudding nurse with a little bowl of something golden.

'Could you put this tray up on the locker, please, Nurse?'

'What's happened to your poor voice?'

'Nothing's the same.'

'What about pudding?'

'Put it on the tray for me, please.'

'Get into it later, will you?'

'When I've had a drink.'

'Will I pour you some?'

'Thanks.'

She has a mouthful of the drink, reaches out and puts the glass back on the locker. She removes two pillows and lies down to sleep.

'We left you, dear, let you sleep. Now we'll get you tidied up. You got visitors coming?'

'Yes.'

'That's nice. Let them do the talking. Look after that throat of yours. You can just nod and smile, like the Queen. We'll wheel you over the other side first, by the window. Right? Then we'll get you out onto the chair for a few minutes while we make your bed. And you'll have time for a little wash and a brush up. We're bringing you a room-mate later.'

'Good.'

Out of the window there are rows of petunias, many times darker than what she's known. They are purple-black, black-blue, red-black, brown-black and black. She won't ask what's happened to colours.

Trolley. A gowned, masked nurse is pulling on gloves.

'We'll put a catheter in, dear. You'll feel better after that, able to get a good night's rest. Have you been at all since . . . ?'

'No.'

'Did they try you out on the chair?'

'Mmmm.'

'Run the tap?'

'Yes.'

'What about the lav, did they take you down?'

'After visiting.'

'Not much voice there . . . Now this won't hurt . . . that's it, we're in business. Well now! No voice, no plumbing, how's the rest of it?'

'Healing up fine, Mr Siers said.' It was one of the things she could safely say: 'Yes.' 'No.' 'No voice.' 'Healing up fine.'

'Crikey, I should've brought a drum down to flow you off into. I've filled one bottle, and now this one's halfway. Must've been sore, poor you. Anyway, should feel a lot better after this . . . I know what, I'll get one of the nurses to bring a bowl in when I've finished and you can have a little wash. You can get pretty sweaty and worried having bits and pieces poked in, taken out, tubes all over the place . . . Taking it out now. That's it. How does it feel?'

'Much better.'

'And tomorrow they'll have you walking a bit more. Then you'll be away laughing, what do you think?'

'There'll be no stopping me.'

'Good on you. Now me, I'm taking this lot away, and going to get me out of this gear. Have a good sleep. And anyway, they'll give you something, won't they, to help you sleep?' Her voice floats back from the corridor above the noise of the trolley.

'Nurse'll be along with a bowl – for a wash. Goodnight.'

In the morning she doesn't know whether she has slept or not. She has the feeling of not having slept, of having listened for many hours to the groans and mutterings of the woman next to her, of having been aware of the night nurses coming in, playing the torches discreetly over the two of them.

'I came in with a nose bleed,' the woman says, 'and they did a Caesarean.' The woman has been propped up on pillows and she lies back against them with her eyes closed. Her fingers play along the edge of the counterpane. It's a relief to hear the woman speak.

'What did you have?'

'A girl. I think she's dying.' Tears run down from under the woman's closed lids.

'What did they say?'

'They're doing their best. They'll wheel me down . . .'

The woman begins to breathe deeply as though she's fallen asleep again.

Later that morning she is taken to the lavatory to perch and a few drops of urine leak away.

'That's only spillage,' the nurse says, 'not the real thing.' She's little and rosy and talkative. 'Lean back, relax as much as you can.'

So she lets herself sag, deepens her breathing, waits.

'You can leave me here if you like.'

'No, we'll give it another couple of minutes. Don't want you pegging out on us.' It's true that she's feeling dizzy. 'If it's no go, we'll get you back to bed. You can drink some more fizz, have another cup of tea.'

When she gets back into the room the woman is being helped back into bed.

'How's baby?'

'It's sad for a baby to just lie there, with no one,' the woman says.

'What did they say when you . . . ?'

'Next twelve hours should tell . . . Just tubes, sticking plaster, things . . . Just a tiny baby, in a little glass bed.' The woman's voice becomes a whisper.

She turns to look out the window. What did it matter about flowers, about colours, when there were more important things. You were the only one to tell yourself what you saw. It was only you who knew, so what did it matter. The woman's being there was helping her – the woman's night moaning and snoring, the tears, the baby, naked, alone, perhaps dying in the little glass canoe.

It was something to think about. It helped, which didn't seem right or fair.

'No clothes for baby,' the woman says. 'Nothing ready. I wasn't even six months. It's never happened like this before. Always gone full term . . .'

'Someone will . . .'

'Not the father, he hasn't been in. Couldn't even find him to bring me here. My nose was pouring, messing my clothes, messing the taxi . . .'

The woman begins to cry again. 'It's just baby's clothes. Without the clothes it's like I'm not expecting . . . to take baby home. There's nothing from the last one. Gave it all away long ago. It's like not expecting baby . . . to live.'

So the woman needed baby clothes so that she could know through the next twelve hours that she was expecting to take her baby home.

'I got clothes,' she says to the woman. 'Two drawers, naps and all. I don't need them.'

The woman is silent, wondering perhaps if the clothes are not needed because a baby has died.

'My baby's eighteen months, walking round, I won't be having more now.'

'I'd like the clothes,' the woman says.

'My cousin's coming in an hour. She could bring them if
I ring.'

'Getting round and taking notice now, are you?' the nurse
asks as she helps her to a phone.

'Are you busting?' the nurse says from behind the trolley, from
behind the mask.

'Feels like it.'

'A bit more voice than yesterday?'

'Yes.'

'Good-oh. Here we go.'

Later that evening two ministers come in to pray with the
woman. They put on purple gowns and mantles.

'I been in to see baby,' one of them says. 'I prayed with
baby. Baby's holding her own. Before that, all afternoon, we
been with the koroua. And after our karakia, going back to pray
with him.'

They begin the prayers, and somewhere beyond the window
a bird starts to squeal intermittently. The chanting is restful. She
doesn't hear the ministers leave.

The woman hasn't slept. 'The bird kept on all night, now it's
gone.' Only her lips move. Then there's movement in the
doorway, a glimpse of purple in the half-dark.

'Kua mate te koroua,' the minister says, and moves away.

'I thought it was baby. Instead it was the koroua. When
I heard the bird I thought it was a message about baby. I suppose if it was baby they would have come for me. I was waiting
for them to come.'

'Who's the old man they're talking about?'

'From up home. Last year we had his ninetieth birthday,
up home. Tino ngawari te koroua ra, real gentle.' Tears slide
across the woman's temples and into her hair.

'Last night, in the night, I was glad about the clothes.'

'Great, that's wonderful.'

'Only a trickle.'

'Two trickles and a drop, but you're on your way. Away laughing. Perch there and concentrate for a while and we'll see what happens.'

She waits. Finally she is peeing into the bowl, forever.

'Milestones,' the nurse says. 'And they take out a few clips in the morning. Right?'

'Right.'

'You'll be a box of birds when I come back on tomorrow.'

There's a world spinning, dust-covered, where stick people search, finding nothing.

People are calling her name.

People calling.

Someone . . . wiping her face.

'Passed out on us, love? Not too pleasant getting the clips out. But those were the worst ones. You'll hardly feel the next lot. Mr Siers'll tell you when he comes. Do you want a drink?'

'No thanks.'

'Voice gone on you. A bit shaky are you? Well let's leave you flat like that for a bit, tuck you in so you can have a good rest before visiting.'

She lies flat and straight with the blankets tucked in tightly. The screen curtains make a wall about her, and when she blinks her eyes, dark smudges move about the space like flying clods. Am I here flat and face upwards, or there sitting upright at the edge? Edge? But you do not question. Curiosity can become a plan to escape. From where? From what? You do not question, but instead lie still, planning what ordinary things to say to visitors, ordinary things that help, that keep you where you are.

She tells her visitors about the old man, the woman, the baby, the clothes for the baby, the clips, her voice, her bladder.

They tell her she doesn't look good, that she'd looked better yesterday.

'There could be a draught,' someone says, 'from the window.'

The woman is wiping her face with a towel as she is wheeled back into the room. Her eyes are red and puffy.

'It's good what they can do,' the woman says as she's helped into bed.

'Is baby all right?'

'She's pulling through. They said she's a strong little thing . . . As long as nothing develops. But . . . they lost one this morning.' The woman begins to cry again. 'The mother never held him . . . alive. The family didn't . . . We talked about our babies yesterday, the other mother and me. Yesterday she sent her husband off to get a bassinet. It was like me with the clothes. You have to have baby's things, a name for baby, otherwise it's like waiting to see.'

For some time the woman is quiet, then she says, 'Before I saw her I called her Cynthia. Don't know why. It's not a family name. It just came, out of nowhere, but I wanted her to have a name. She had to be somebody, with a name, with clothes. So I been calling her Cynthia when I go down.'

'Did it suit her, when you saw her?'

'Suits her good. Cynthia suits her just right. Father mightn't like it, but too bad, she's already Cynthia.'

She wants the woman to go on talking.

'Who does she look like then?'

'Nobody, just herself. She's tiny, but got big hands, like our other girls – long hands, with long, pointy fingers. The other one, the one that died this morning, was little, like Cynthia, but had tiny, tiny hands.'

Was that it then? Was it the long-hands people who inherited the earth? Was it the tiny-hands people who escaped? No. Keep talking.

'Is your bladder okay today?' the woman asks.

'Dribble dribble, but it's better than nothing.'
'And your voice's gone funny again.'
'Fix up one end, then the other end packs up.'
'I'm getting some clips out in a day or two . . .'
'It's no picnic . . .'
'But I don't seem to care about anything. I don't even want to look outside.'

She decides then that she will tell the woman.

'They put me over here so I could look out,' she says, 'I couldn't believe . . . the flowers were all strange, and different-coloured. Dark and bright. I got scared.'

The woman doesn't speak.

'All the flowers, these ones too. And the food. Strange. I was scared, but now . . . I don't care.'

'At night,' the woman says, 'there's people come and sit on me, on my feet, on my chest.'

'I thought they'd ripped fish out of my guts, dragged them up my throat, out of my mouth.'

'It's tubes. They do it to babies too . . . People, every night, and I stay still, keep myself awake, until they go.'

'Sometimes I see what it might be like outside, now, or some other time. There are two of me. One showing the other, making her see. It could be a dream, but it's more like seeing. It *is* seeing. It's like a world with nothing. People with no kai, no clothes, nothing. Just dirt.'

'I been trying to grow a garden, and the only thing good is turnips.' The woman sits forward in her bed smiling. 'And tomatoes. I had a real good crop. Ha!'

So it's all right. She's told the woman and the woman hasn't seemed surprised, hasn't noticed, possibly hasn't heard.

She watches the woman lean back into the pillows.

'But I don't really want to think about the garden,' the woman says, 'or home, or anything out there. Most of the time I lay here and think about Cynthia, wait for them to tell me how she's doing, wait for them to take me down. I've got this idea that if I don't think about Cynthia she might slip. Don't want to sleep at night. And . . . when *they* come in the night

I don't know if it's good or bad, if they help me – or if they've come for Cynthia. I just wait . . . just keep awake. After a while they go.'

'Do you see?'

'Only feel.'

'Who is it, then?'

'Don't know. People belonging to me, the old people, I suppose. Anyway, it wouldn't be strangers. So I wait it out, keep my mind on Cynthia and just wait.'

In the quiet that follows they hear the trolleys at the other end of the corridor.

'You been eating,' the woman says, 'this morning, I noticed.'

'I tried to eat most of it, then missed lunch. The food looks plastic, and different . . .'

'You been having a hard time.'

'At first I was scared, but not now, because I know I'm really as tough as guts. Underneath I'm as tough as guts. No, it's you. You're the one who's having a hard time. It's different . . . if it's a baby.'

'Cynthia's coming through. She's strong. But I can't help crying, because it's like she has to make it on her own . . . no mother, no family, no clothes on her, no blanket – just machines, tubes, sticking plaster. Anyway it's only machines and tubes that's kept her going, it's good what they can do. I suppose they wonder why I'm always crying my eyes out.'

Cold meat, lettuce salad, tomato and two slices of bread. She finds she can put colour on, or take it off. There's a trick to it. It doesn't matter because later she'll stop doing it, stop being able to do it. She'll be home, too busy to think about it. She's determined to eat the food, and takes a bite out of the slice of bread. While she's eating she'll talk to the woman . . . about tomatoes.

'We had a good crop too, tomatoes. Must've been a good year.'

'I was out picking,' the woman says, 'and that's when my nose bled, pouring like a river.'

Red. Blood, fruit, river. What can she do? What should she

do? She wants to scream, to go to the woman, ask what it's all about. Where are we? What can we do?

'Blood pressure's good now,' the woman says, 'right back to normal.'

'Good. That's good.'

She will eat – cut the tomato and eat it, cut up the meat, chew, swallow. While she's eating she'll talk to the woman. In a couple of days she'll go home.

The skirt is too big but she pins a tuck in it. She puts on her coat and shoes.

'I can go too, in three days,' the woman says. 'I'll come in each day until I can take Cynthia home.'

'How long before . . . ?'

'It could be another three weeks.'

'Cynthia's doing fine.'

'She's strong.'

'We'll meet again one day.'

'We will.'

She walks the long corridor wearing a warm coat over a pinned-up skirt, passing window after window, like watching a train. There's rain on the windows. She looks down on old buildings, a busy road. She descends in a noiseless lift and walks along more corridors.

At the door she feels the cool air on her face. There's slanting rain, and she walks out on to wet pathways between beds of glossy flowers and shrubs, to the car. The wheels turn on wet asphalt, swishing through the rain. And she thinks that only the rain and sun know that buildings can become rubble, that roads can become dust, that somewhere along the road are people, bare as bone, turning each stone and each grain.

Ahead of them is one corner, and another, and another. All she wants for now is to come to each one blindly – and not to know what is round this bend, the next, the next one after that.

More about Penguins

For further information about books available from Penguin please write to the following:

In New Zealand: For a complete list of books available from Penguin in New Zealand write to the Marketing Department, Penguin Books (N.Z.) Ltd, Private Bag, Takapuna, Auckland.

In Australia: For a complete list of books available from Penguin in Australia write to the Marketing Department, Penguin Books Australia Ltd, P.O. Box 257, Ringwood, Victoria 3134.

In Britain: For a complete list of books available from Penguin in Britain write to Dept EP, Penguin Books Ltd, Harmondsworth, Middlesex UB7 ODA.

In the U.S.A.: For a complete list of books available from Penguin in the United States write to Dept DG, Penguin Books, 299 Murray Hill Parkway, East Rutherford, New Jersey 07073.

In Canada: For a complete list of books available from Penguin in Canada write to Penguin Books Canada Ltd, 2801 John Street, Markham, Ontario L3R 1B4.

Patricia Grace in Penguins

POTIKI

Winner of third equal prize in the 1986 Wattie Book of the Year Awards.

'*Potiki* could be the most important New Zealand novel published in 1986. It explores themes of challenge and response in the life of a small Maori community threatened by coastal development for tourism. . . . It is as rich and plausible a cross-section of a rural Maori community as I've met in fiction; it integrates rural-urban Maori themes more successfully than any book previously published; it reveals the action of mythology at work in twentieth-century Maori life in a manner that would surprise most Pakeha, especially those currently setting out to discredit psychic phenomena as mere showmanship; it evokes a relationship between land and the people who live on it; and it shows the action of the past continuously at work upon the present.'
Michael King, *Auckland Metro*

'Patricia Grace's writing is as delicate as Japanese brushwork, yet as poignant and throat-aching as the loss of a loved one. Her latest novel, *Potiki*, is an expression of what we in Aotearoa are — loving, caring, sometimes greedy and vengeful, forgiving, optimistic. . . . There is a many-sided symbolism in this story which Maori people will warm to, for every incident has significance. It is like a never-ending discovery of the many-dimensional nature of mankind.'
Arapera Blank, *N.Z. Listener*

'It will, perhaps, help Pakeha people to a better understanding of matters Maori. It will also help many Maori people to a better understanding of themselves.'
Te Paki Cherrington, *N.Z. Herald*

'Every marketeer and property developer in the country deserves a copy of *Potiki*. Patricia Grace sees straight, but are we listening?'
Sue McCauley, *N.Z. Listener*

'*Potiki* by Patricia Grace is, without doubt, the book I enjoyed most this year. Delicate in its blend of prose and poetry, yet powerful in its statement of cultural identity, this chronicle of a Maori whanau expertly weaves together the timelessness of Maori mythology with contemporary

political realities. Although *Potiki* is significant for me for its affirmation and reflection of familiar cultural images, it has wider appeal with its deep emotional moral and social content.'
Miriama Evans, *The Dominion*

'The New Zealand author tells a vivid and mesmerizing story as she blends tribal myth with political realities and offers shrewd insights into human nature. The unique book is also full of exotic symbolism and language.
. . .'
Publishers Weekly (U.S.A.)

WAIARIKI
and other stories

Patricia Grace's popular first collection – sensitive stories of Maori life which explore Maori spirituality and values and pursue relationships between people, families and races.

'For me, Patricia's stories have a haunting loveliness. My responses to them vary from shrieks of delight, to solemn agreement, to tears, to acceptance.'
Keri Kaa

'Patricia Grace meets Pakeha attitudes to Maori head on, without anger.'
Marilyn Duckworth, *N.Z. Listener*

'A series of penetrating observations of everyday activities, such as cooking or fishing, a sudden movement, a momentary glance or snatches of conversation. . . . Every incident, every little detail, so unpretentious, so warmly portrayed, is quite evidently the work of a writer who understands and appreciates every aspect of her subject.'
Margaret Lawler, *Auckland Star*

MUTUWHENUA
The Moon Sleeps

'Stainless and shining, and as pure as the night of Mutuwhenua when the moon goes underground and sleeps.'

This is the story of Ripeka, who leaves her extended family and its traditional lifestyle to marry Graeme, a Pakeha schoolteacher. In the strange world of the city Ripeka discovers that she cannot make the spiritual break, that the old ways are too strong.

'There is an air of innocence that permeates Patricia Grace's writing which, in the harsh light of today's realities, gives *Mutuwhenua* an unworldly, almost fairytale quality. . . . The emotions of compassion and gentleness so skilfully evoked in these pages will, I feel sure, remain with many readers for a long time.'
N.Z. Bookworld

THE DREAM SLEEPERS
and other stories

Stories of family life in the country and the city, of the contrasts between young and old, of relationships between people who know what it means to be Maori in a society whose predominant values are alien.

'Grace is simply the best short-story writer to have emerged in this country in the last decade.'
N.Z. Listener

'Patricia Grace has almost entirely (not absolutely) avoided the schmaltzy sentimentality of so many stories of childhood or family. Instead, she conveys with clarity in some of these stories the complexes of colliding emotions people experience, as those of the mother in childbirth – the awake dreams of a whole variety of characters.'
Bernard Gadd

'One of those rare books you'll want to re-read straight away.'
Tu Tangata